Just For ~~Tonight~~ Forever

D.E. Haggerty

Copyright © 2022 D.E. Haggerty

All rights reserved.

D.E. Haggerty asserts the moral right to be identified as the author of this work.

ISBN: 9798835193806

Just For Forever is a work of fiction. The names, characters, places, and incidents portrayed in it are the product of the author's imagination. Any resemblance to actual persons, living or dead, events or locations is entirely coincidental.

All rights reserved. No part of this publication may be reproduced, stored in a retrieval system, or transmitted, in any form or by any means, electronic, mechanical, photocopying, recording or otherwise, without the prior permission of the author.

No portion of this book may be reproduced in any form without written permission from the publisher or author, except as permitted by U.S. copyright law.

Also by D.E. Haggerty

My Forever Love
Forever For You
Stay For Forever
Only Forever
Meet Disaster
Meet Not
Meet Dare
Meet Hate
Bragg's Truth
Bragg's Love
Perfect Bragg
Bragg's Match
Bragg's Christmas
How to Date a Rockstar
How to Love a Rockstar
How to Fall For a Rockstar
A Hero for Hailey
A Protector for Phoebe
A Soldier for Suzie

A Fox for Faith
A Christmas for Chrissie
A Valentine for Valerie
A Love for Lexi
About Face
At Arm's Length
Hands Off
Knee Deep
Molly's Misadventures

Chapter One

Four months ago

"Excuse me."

At the sound of a man's husky voice, I halt rummaging through the cleaning supplies. Holy hot flashes. A man's voice should not be sexy enough on its own to cause a shiver to run down my spine, but that's exactly what's happening.

I need to see the face that matches the voice. Since I'm on my knees with my butt sticking out of the supply closet, I stand and whirl around at the same time. Unfortunately, I forgot I was holding onto a box of cleaning supplies and Mr. Sexy Voice is standing directly behind me. The box collides with his body, and I lose my hold on it causing it to drop to the floor and the contents to fly out and scatter through the hallway.

"Shit," I mutter as I drop to my knees to gather the supplies.

"Let me help." He offers.

I look up to tell him not to worry about it and – whack! – our heads collide since he's already leaning over. I fall back on my bottom and place a hand on my head. Ow.

"I wasn't looking forward to my trip to a small town, but I didn't expect to get injured the second I arrive."

I scowl up at him – small towns are awesome, especially if the small town is Winter Falls – but the scowl freezes on my face when I get my first look at him. Yowzah! Talk about a stone cold fox. His dark hair is styled to appear as if he just rolled out of bed – making me itch to run my fingers through it and mess up all the careful styling – while his deep, blue eyes sparkle with humor as he watches me check him out. And then there's his jaw. Square jaws are like catnip to me. I want to caress his jaw while I kiss him.

He chuckles and I remember where I am – sitting on my ass in the hallway at my bed and breakfast. What is wrong with me? I'm not usually klutzy Karen, and I do NOT check out guests. I mentally slap myself upside the head. Get yourself together, woman. No drooling over a strange man no matter how sexy his voice is.

I ignore his hand offering to help me up and stand on my own. When I reach my full height of a whopping five-feet-two, I realize this man is not only gorgeous but tall. Probably around six-foot. I would fit perfectly snuggled under his shoulder. So much for not drooling over strange men.

I shut the supply closet door behind me and walk around the reception desk. "Checking in?"

"Won't your boss get mad at you for checking me in? Maybe you should call him."

Him? I briefly close my eyes to stop myself from rolling them. Rolling eyes at guests is bad, even when they are being presumptuous.

"It's fine. *She* won't mind." I make sure to emphasize the *she* as I wiggle the mouse to wake up the computer and type in my password. "Do you have a reservation?"

He doesn't respond and I gaze up at him to discover him staring at me. I know I don't look my best. Rushing around trying to clean all the rooms in the inn after getting up early to prepare breakfast doesn't exactly equal a fresh and clean appearance. My face is probably red and shiny, and I don't want to think about how my hair looks.

"Do you have a reservation?" I repeat my question.

He finally snaps out of his silence and nods. "Yes. It's under Cole Hawkins."

Dang. A sexy name for a sexy man.

"Are you positive your boss—"

"Here, it is," I say and cut him off.

I should probably tell him I'm the owner and operator of the *Inn on Main* at this point, but it'll be more fun to let him figure it out on his own. And I could use some fun.

"You'll be staying with us for two weeks?"

"Yes."

"I've put you in the executive suite on the top floor. You won't …" My words trail off as the Chief of Police stalks into the building.

"Chief Alston." My voice sounds friendly, but there's a frown on my face. I always assumed Lyric would become my brother-in-law since my older sister, Aspen, has been in love with him forever, but the two broke up a decade ago and my sister's been heartbroken ever since.

Being a witness to Lyric moving on with his life and dating other women has been painful, especially since my sister avoids coming home because she's afraid to see him with another woman. She'll deny it, but I know it's true.

He nods to me in greeting before focusing his attention on my guest. "Are you the owner of the Jeep Grand Cherokee?"

Uh oh. Someone's in trouble.

Cole's eyebrows pinch together. "I am. Is there a problem? Don't tell me someone ran into my car. It's brand new."

I giggle. Who exactly would have run into his car? The transportation method of choice in Winter Falls is a golf cart. Although I suppose a golf cart could cause some damage to a Jeep. My baby sister, Ashlyn, managed to scratch the heck out of a police car when she lost control of a golf cart while racing down the street when she was in high school.

Lyric places his hands on his hips and glares at Cole. "Did you receive dispensation to drive the car into Winter Falls?"

"Dispensation? What are you talking about?"

Winter Falls' claim to fame is being the first carbon neutral town in the world. As such, we have a bunch of rules and regulations about energy use including driving cars in town.

Lyric switches his glare to me. "Aren't guests informed of the rules regarding gas-guzzling vehicles when they book a room at the inn?"

Cole stands in front of me. "Hey! Don't give her a hard time. She's merely a cleaner here."

Lyric cocks his eyebrow. I know he's wondering why I haven't corrected Cole's misconceptions, but I don't answer to him. It's none of his business I'm giving Cole a lesson in how to treat people. It's also none of his business how I practically melted at Cole's protective stance.

"You need a dispensation to drive a gas engine vehicle in Winter Falls," Lyric explains to Cole when I don't speak.

Cole scratches his neck. "I do? How do visitors arrive if not by car? Is there a bus or railroad station?"

He's got a point. As much as Winter Falls likes to pretend it's an island, it's not. There aren't exactly islands the size of this town in the middle of the Colorado foothills.

No matter how much food we produce locally, there are tons of necessities we can't produce such as toilet paper. Trust me, toilet paper is a necessity. I am done trying to teach the world how to use a bidet.

It's officially no longer my fight. Toilet paper is a must have and it needs to reach Winter Falls somehow.

But why is Lyric being such an ass? Normally, he doesn't show up at the inn to harass guests about the vehicles they used to arrive in town with. As long as the vehicle remains parked behind the inn for the duration of their stay, it's fine. But he's got a bug up his ass today.

And I think I know why. "You saw Aspen." It's not a question.

He frowns. "Did you know she was coming back to town?"

Of course, I knew. Her bookstore and apartment in Dallas burned down a few days ago. Where else was she going to go? But we agreed to keep her return secret because my big sister asked us to. Keeping a secret in this town is akin to a miracle, but we managed.

"Why don't I get you a cup of coffee and a cookie?" I round the desk and walk to the small refreshment station in the lobby before he has a chance to answer.

I prepare a cup of coffee for him and place a cookie on a plate.

"I don't—"

I don't let Lyric finish whatever denial he was planning to give me and press the items in his hands.

"Sit. Take a load off for a while. I'll get Mr. Hawkins checked in and then I'll join you."

His chin drops to his chest, and he takes a seat.

I turn to my guest. "Do you need help with your baggage?" He shakes his head. "I'll show you to your room then."

I swipe the room key from the desk and begin ascending the stairs. "The execute suite is on the third floor. Breakfast in the morning is from—"

"Was he serious?" He cuts me off to ask.

"Who serious about what?"

"The chief of police. Was he serious about needing dispensation for my car? What kind of crazy town is this?"

I bristle at his question. Is Winter Falls a bit kooky? Of course, it is. The town was founded by a group of hippies. How can it not be kooky? But it's also a fun place to live and there's not one person in this town of a thousand and one people who I wouldn't trust to have my back. I can't imagine living anywhere else.

"There's no need for concern. You are free to drive your car to and from town. Within town, however, you should either walk, bike, or use a golf cart. Bikes and golf carts are free to borrow. There are stations with them scattered throughout town, including behind the inn."

We reach his room, and I motion for him to proceed me. The executive suite is one of my favorite rooms. It's not technically a 'suite' as the bedroom is not a separate room and there isn't a kitchen area. But there is a separate living space and a desk set up in front of the large window with a view over Main Street.

"I'm here for work," Cole says. "I need my car to get to meetings."

I barely hold in my eye roll. He 'needs' his car. Where exactly are his meetings? You can literally walk from one side of Winter Falls to the other in less than twenty minutes.

"What kind of work are you here for?"

He puffs out his chest. "I'm an architect."

"You're here for the community center project." It's not a question. In a small town – especially this small town – everyone knows what's going on.

"I'm surprised you've heard about it."

Why is he surprised? Oh yeah. He thinks I'm a cleaner. "I'm actually—"

He cuts me off before I have a chance to tell him how I actually own *The Inn on Main*. "I guess you must have heard about it from your boss."

I open my mouth to once again try to clear up the misunderstanding happening here, but Cole is on a roll.

"Anyway, I'm an architect." Yes, you said. "And my firm is bidding to acquire the project. I'll be meeting with the mayor and city council."

"The plot for the community center isn't far from here. It's not even a five-minute walk."

"You're well-informed for your position."

I don't bother trying to clear up his misconception again. I tried. I failed. I'd much rather have a front row seat when he realizes the truth. Someone's going to be mighty embarrassed. Not my problem. It's not my fault making assumptions makes you an ass.

Chapter Two

When I reach the reception area, Lyric is gone as is the cookie I gave him. I take the plate and coffee cup to the kitchen before exiting through the back door of the bed and breakfast. My sister, Aspen, should be arriving at our parents' house any moment now and I want to be there to welcome her back home.

She thinks she's only here for a visit while she waits for the insurance company to pay her claim for the business and home that burnt down. She doesn't realize the entire town is planning on doing everything within our power to make her stay. Game on.

I walk to my parents' house since nothing is far in Winter Falls. I wave at my sisters, Ashlyn, Lilac, and Juniper, waiting with my parents on the front porch for Aspen to arrive. Mom and Dad had five daughters. Aspen's the oldest. I'm next. Two years behind me is Lilac. Then, they took a four-year break until Juniper came along. And, finally, there's the baby cakes of the family, Ashlyn.

My mom wraps her arm around my shoulders as soon as I'm within range. "Ellery Promise." She rocks me back and forth. "Have you met any hot men at the inn lately?"

I groan. "Seriously? The guy checked in five minutes ago. How can you possibly know about him already?"

"A mother knows all," she sings. "Don't forget to use protection."

"I'm not going to sleep with him," I protest despite my body tingling in anticipation at the idea. I've obviously been working too hard. I don't tingle when thinking about a man whom I just met. Men aren't on my radar. Work and making the inn a success is all I care about.

"Why not? From what I heard, he's scrumptious."

"Ew! Stop." Ashlyn feigns gagging.

"I don't know why you're such a prude," Mom tells her. "It's like you're not my daughter."

"Maybe I got switched at the hospital at birth." Ashlyn wiggles her eyebrows.

"Except you have my eyes and your father's height." Ashlyn's shoulders slump. "And you never left my sight in the hospital."

"Speaking of wayward daughters," Dad interrupts to gesture toward the tow truck barreling down the street.

"What is Aspen doing in Basil's Beast?" I wonder.

"I assume her car broke down," Lilac answers.

"I meant ..." I cut myself off. There's no sense in explaining myself to Lilac. She takes everything literally.

The tow truck pulls into the driveaway and Mom rushes down the porch and wrenches the passenger door open. "Aspen Cloud, you're home." She wraps her arms around Aspen and sways her from side to side. "I can't tell you how happy I am to see you."

Aspen melts into Mom. Huh. My big sister doesn't usually accept the comfort our mom so freely offers. She must be more stressed than she let on when I talked to her before she began her journey from Texas to Colorado. I'm not judging. I'd be stressed out of my freaking mind if the inn burned down, and the insurance company blamed me.

"You're going to be fine, baby girl. Just fine," Mom tells her.

"Thanks, Mom."

Dad elbows Mom out of the way and lifts Aspen before twirling her around. She giggles as he spins her.

"Put me down, Dad. I'm not a child," she claims despite continuing to giggle like one.

Dad sets her on the ground and whispers something to her too soft for me to hear.

"Stop hogging her!" I scream before Juniper, Lilac, Ashlyn, and I rush down the front porch and jump Aspen. We're rolling on the ground in no time.

"It's good to have you home, big sis," I tell her while my other sisters murmur their agreement.

Woof!

Aspen struggles to my feet. "I need to let Waffles out before he pees all over the interior of my car."

Lilac curls her lip at the state of Aspen's car. "This is your vehicle? It's in violation of the town ordinance."

Aspen rolls her eyes. "Yes, Ms. Know It All, but I didn't exactly have a ton of cash laying around to buy a car when my life burned to the ground. Literally."

Lilac flinches. "Sorry, Aspen. I didn't mean ..." She clears her throat. "Anyway, I assume Basil will be removing this eyesore from the driveway."

"Geez, Lilac. Have some compassion." Ashlyn bumps her shoulder as she passes her to open the passenger door of Aspen's car.

Waffles jumps out of the car, dashes to the lawn, does three circles, and promptly lifts his leg to have a wee. He barks when he notices a squirrel on the lawn and rushes after it. Except he's still peeing. Pee streams out of him, splashing his legs and paws, as he runs.

The squirrel scurries up a tree, and Waffles paws at the tree while barking up a storm at the poor squirrel. At least, he's finally done peeing.

"I got him," Juniper – the animal lover of us – yells. "You unload the car."

She holds out a treat to Waffles and his attention swivels away from the tree toward her. She keeps the treat out in front of her as she backs into the house with Aspen's dog eagerly following her. I wish she'd wash him before allowing him in the house.

"Is this everything?" Dad asks from where he's peering into Aspen's trunk.

"Yeah," Aspen sighs.

I wrap my arm around her. "It could have been worse." Judging by her scowl, she doesn't believe me. I squeeze her shoulder. "You're alive. You're young and you can rebuild."

"Easy for you to say. You have a successful business. I have nothing."

"Yeah, well, owning a B&B is not all it's cracked up to be," I mutter under my breath. Especially not when guests talk down to the cleaner. There is absolutely nothing wrong with cleaning for a living. And why wouldn't a cleaner be informed about what's happening in town? Stupid, gorgeous jerk.

Once Aspen's car – referring to the decrepit thing as a car is pushing it – is empty and all her things have been placed in her childhood bedroom, we gather at the dining room table where Mom has an apple pie waiting for us. Mom thinks apple pie heals all wounds. Her pie kind of does.

"What happened?" Ashlynn asks. "Why did your bookstore and apartment burn down?"

Typical baby sister. She blurts out whatever she's thinking without considering a person's feelings first.

I squeeze Aspen's hand. "You don't have to answer her."

"It's fine," she claims but swallows as if it's painful. She wasn't hurt, was she? "Waffles woke me up in the middle of the night because he needed to go out. When we returned, flames were shooting out of the café and bookstore downstairs. I rushed upstairs and managed to throw some clothes and jewelry in a suitcase and put some of my photo albums and books in a few boxes."

"You went into a burning building?" Dad roars.

"Only the ground floor was actually burning. There weren't any flames in my apartment above."

"You could have been killed."

At his words, Aspen draws the sleeves of her t-shirt down over her hands. Before I have a chance to ask what happened, Mom shackles her wrist and carefully draws the material up her arm.

Mom's bottom lip trembles and there are tears in her eyes when she notices the bandages covering Aspen's lower arms. "You didn't tell us you were injured."

"It's fine. They're barely second-degree burns."

"Second-degree burns can cause scarring," Lilac offers. When everyone at the table glares at her, her eyes round. "What? It's a fact. You can't get mad at me for stating facts." She's an environmental engineer, not a doctor, but her brain is full of all kinds of random facts. Great for when she's on your pub quiz team, less great when she forgets the word tact exists in the dictionary.

Aspen sighs. "I'm not mad at you, Lilac Bean."

Except she used Lilac's middle name. The West sisters only refer to each other by our middle names if we're annoyed with each other. Not one of us likes our hippie middle name. It's bad enough our first names are all trees.

Mom stands. "Let me phone Dr. Blue. I'm certain we can get you an appointment right away."

"There's no need. I've seen a doctor. He gave me antibiotics. Everything's fine."

Mom looks to Lilac for confirmation. At her nod, Mom returns to the table. "But you need to promise to tell me if you're in pain."

"I promise."

"Now," my dad says once the pie is demolished, "tell me why your insurance company won't pay out your claim."

Dad may appear to be a laidback hippie most of the time, but he's also the town's attorney. And he doesn't let anyone mess with his girls.

Aspen shrugs. "Since the cause of the fire is unclear, they need to conduct an arson investigation and eliminate me as a suspect before they'll pay my claim."

"Are they out of their minds?" Dad bellows.

Mom pats his arm. "Now, now, Daniel. Getting your heart rate up will not help the situation." "Besides," she smirks at Aspen, "our baby girl is home until the insurance company pays the claim."

I frown at Mom. She wasn't supposed to tell Aspen we're planning to convince her to stay in town, but she practically announced it from the rooftops with her smirk. Dang it. It's going to be hard enough persuading my big sister to stay. And now Mom's gone and made it harder.

Chapter Three

*C*ole

My leg bounces up and down as I sit in the breakfast room of the country inn and drink my coffee. I'm trying my best to remain calm but it's difficult when the most important appointment of my career is nearly upon me. If I can land the contract to build the community center in Winter Falls, I'll be one step closer to reaching my dream of making partner at *Davis Williams* before I turn thirty-five next year.

Lucky for me, Winter Falls wants an environmentally sustainable building, and I specialize in passive heating and cooling systems. This is my chance to make a name for myself. I can't screw it up.

I check my watch and realize I have thirty minutes before my appointment with the mayor. I set my coffee cup down and stand. Time to make my dreams come true.

I stroll down Main Street toward the plot on which the community center will be built. I pass a jewelry store, *Bohemian Treasures,* before reaching the empty lot next door. The scent of coffee and donuts hits me, and I scan the area for the source. Next door is *Bake Me Happy*. Are all of the shop names wacky in this town?

"You must be Cole," a voice booms from behind and startles me.

This is it. My big chance. I take a deep breath and force myself to relax before pivoting to greet the man.

My eyes widen as I take in his appearance. He's tall and sports a long, unkept beard. Whereas I'm wearing my best suit for the meeting, he's in jeans and a t-shirt. Both of which should have been thrown out ages ago. Probably before I was born.

My eyes widen further when I realize he's holding a leash and on the end of the leash is a squirrel. I blink but when my vision clears there's still a squirrel sitting there. And I thought the shop names were wacky.

I hold out my hand. "And you must be Mr. Forest."

"Just Forest. No Mr. We don't stand on pretense in Winter Falls," he tells me as we shake hands. "Tell me about yourself."

"I'm an architect with the firm *Davis Williams.*"

He waves a hand. "Not about your job. What about you?"

"Yeah, Mr. Tall Drink of Water. Tell us all about you."

I whirl around to find a group of elderly women giving me the once-over. "Hello," I greet despite having the feeling I should be running away.

Another woman rushes over to join them. "Did you start without me?"

One of the women rolls her eyes. "We wouldn't dare, Sage."

"Are you ladies members of the city council?" I ask and hope they say no.

They giggle. "He's a polite one saying we're ladies."

"We are ladies."

One of them snorts. "Like hell we are."

"This is Feather, Petal, Sage, Cayenne, and Clove." Forest points to each of them in turn as he introduces them.

I smile at them, and they fan their faces.

"I hope Ellery takes him for a test drive," Feather says.

"Lord knows the girl works entirely too hard. She could use a little relief. If you get my meaning." Sage waggles her eyebrows.

"Who's Ellery?" I interject before one of them decides to explain what they mean by a little relief.

I'm holding onto my professionalism by a thin thread. I might lose hold if this group of women old enough to be grandmothers start talking about sex. Sex I'm supposed to be having with a woman I don't know.

"You must have met her," Forest says. "She owns the inn."

"Oh. I haven't met the owner yet. Just the cleaner yesterday when I checked in."

When I arrived and saw the woman bent over and searching the closet, I nearly lost my mind. My hands reached forward of their own accord to grab hold of her perfect heart-shaped ass. When she landed on her ass in the hallway and looked up at me, I discovered she's gorgeous in addition to sexy.

Despite her obvious embarrassment, her bright, green eyes sparkled with humor while her plush lips I want to taste kicked up in a half-smile. Add in the freckles across a slightly upturned nose and she has the appearance of the girl next door all grown up. What fun it would be to dirty up her fresh faced appearance.

"Should we tell him?" Cayenne asks and ruins my daydream of dirtying the woman up.

"No way. It'll be more fun for him to figure it out for himself," Clove says.

My curiosity is piqued. "Figure what out?"

They mimic zipping their lips. I raise an eyebrow at Forest. "The cleaner you met yesterday is Ellery, the owner."

"Forest! You numbskull. We weren't going to tell him!" Sage smacks his shoulder.

Shit. I feel my face heat as I recall the things I said to her yesterday. I was being a bit of an ass. In my defense, I was already nervous about today's meeting and hadn't expected to be confronted with the most gorgeous creature I've ever seen. The combination of nerves and arousal had me spouting off from the mouth like a complete jerk.

I inhale fresh air and push my embarrassment away. I'll apologize later. For now, I need to get this meeting back on track.

"Shall we go over the drawings we've prepared for the bid?" I ask Forest.

"If they're going to talk shop, I might as well go back to work," Feather says.

"But I want to hear how he's going to make it up to Ellery." Petal does an honest to goodness pout and sticks out her lower lip.

"I need to get back to the station anyway," Sage says and wanders off. The women follow her.

"Let's get a cup of coffee and go through the drawings. I have questions." Forest marches off in the direction of the bakery and I rush to follow him. I expect the staff to protest him bringing a pet squirrel inside, but no one says a thing.

For the next hour, I answer all kinds of questions about the drawings. I don't lose patience, although it's tested when the squirrel jumps on the table and starts nibbling on the drawings. Forest merely chuckles and pets the animal in response while I resist the urge to Google squirrels and communicable diseases.

"Here." The waiter plops a bag down on the table on top of the drawings.

"I didn't order anything."

He winks. "Trust me. Ellery loves these cookies." The owner of the inn Ellery? "They're still warm. Rowan took them out of the oven a minute ago. They're chocolate chip cookies made with oat flour."

I have no idea what oat flour is, but these smell delicious. "Thank you." I think. I'm still confused. Is he helping me apologize? How does he know I need to apologize?

"You're welcome. I'm Bryan by the way. I'm here to handle all of your bakery needs." He flounces off before I have the chance to introduce myself.

As soon as my meeting with Forest ends, I go in search of Ellery to apologize. She's behind the reception desk when I enter the inn. When I observe her this way, it's hard to understand how I could have ever confused the professional woman she obviously is with a cleaner. Her hair is in a tight bun and she's wearing a white blouse and black, pencil skirt. Her appearance screams professional, although the outfit does nothing to detract from how sexy she is.

"Ellery?"

She smiles as she glances my way. The smile dies when she realizes it's me. If there was any doubt as to what kind of first impression I made with her, it's cleared up now. It wasn't good.

"I need to apologize."

She crosses her arms over her chest and my gaze dips to the hint of cleavage revealed. I catch a glimpse of white lace. My blood heats from the tiny view. I wrench my gaze away from her chest. I'm here to apologize not leer at the woman.

"I'm waiting," she says, the amusement clear in her voice.

"I'm sorry. I didn't realize you were the owner when I arrived yesterday. I shouldn't have assumed."

"You know what they say about assumptions," she sings.

I offer her the bakery bag. "I brought an apology gift."

She snatches the bag from me and rips it open before sticking her nose in the bag. "These are still warm."

She stuffs half of a cookie into her mouth and moans. My blood nearly boils over at the sound. I want to hear her make the same sound while I'm devouring her lips.

When she notices me staring at her, she asks, "What? I missed breakfast and it's nearly noon."

I wipe visions of tasting her plush lips from my mind. "Enjoy."

"Did you need anything else? Is there a problem with your room?" she asks when I don't move away.

"The room is lovely." I should have told her that yesterday, but instead, I spouted all kinds of bull crap from my mouth and gave her the impression of being a privileged ass. "I thought I'd ask you out to dinner for a proper apology."

The panic on her face at my question has me back pedaling. "It's not a date. It's an apology dinner. I don't mean to step on any toes if you're dating someone." I check her ring finger. It's bare. "Or if you're married."

"I'm not married or dating anyone, but I prefer to keep my business to myself. A nearly impossible task in a town where gossiping is considered an esteemed hobby."

"I think I understand."

She barks out a laugh. "I forgot you met the royalty of Winter Falls today."

Royalty? Will those old biddies be the ones to decide whether or not *Davis Williams* acquires the contract to build the community center? I hope not. I don't want to think about what kinds of questions they'd ask me. I don't think any of their questions would concern the sustainability of the community center.

"Why don't I cook dinner for you instead?" she offers.

A picture of her stirring a pot at the stove in nothing but an apron showcasing her heart-shaped ass and curvy hips flashes into my mind. I want nothing more than to have her cook me dinner. I clear my throat before offering a token protest. "I don't want to put you out."

She waves away my concern. "It's fine. I enjoy cooking. It's relaxing."

"If you're sure ..."

"I'm more than sure. I live in the old carriage house out back. How does seven sound?"

"Sounds great."

The phone rings and she gives me an apologetic look. "Sorry, I need to ..."

"I'll see you at seven," I say before wandering off to let her get back to work.

Despite the appeal of the community center project, I wasn't excited about the prospect of staying in Winter Falls for two weeks. Small towns are boring. But things are looking up.

Chapter Four

What the hell am I doing? I ask myself as I throw pasta into a pan of boiling water. Why am I making dinner for some guy I barely know? I don't want a man. I don't have time for a man. What has gotten into me? But I couldn't say no to Cole. His blue eyes entranced me, and my mouth offered to cook him dinner at my place before my brain could catch up.

The doorbell rings, and I glance at the kitchen clock. Seven o'clock on the dot. Cole's punctual. Dang. I was counting on him being late. I scan the kitchen counters and the mess I created. I had hoped to have time to clean up before he arrived, but I'm running late. Nothing new for me.

Mom says I was four weeks late when I was born, and I haven't been on time since. She may have a point, but there was no way I was skipping a shower after a full day of work, which included dashing up and down two flights of stairs on a semi-regular basis.

"It's open," I answer as I furiously throw everything on the counter into the sink.

"Hello!" Cole shouts as he enters.

There's no reason to shout. The carriage house is adorable, but it's not very big. It's basically a one-bedroom apartment over a garage.

Since I don't own a car – what use would I have for one? – the garage houses the lawnmower and other gardening equipment.

Although I've tried to make the place feel homey, the apartment isn't much. There's a small kitchen, a tiny 'dining area' – basically a kitchen table stuffed in a corner – and a living room dominated by a corner sofa. The sofa is way too comfortable as evidenced by the number of times I've fallen asleep on it.

I lower the heat on the pasta and dry my hands on a towel before going to greet my guest. My breath catches when I lay my eyes on him. His hair is wet from his shower and without all the product he usually uses, he has adorable curly hair. But his hair isn't why breathing has suddenly become difficult. I blame my lack of air on how his Henley shirt stretches across his broad shoulders. I want to lay my eyes on those shoulders when he isn't wearing a shirt.

"This is a cute place," he says as he scans the area. His words break me out of my fantasy where my hands are roving all over his chest. What can I say? I love a strong chest.

I meet him in the middle of the living room, and he hands me a bag. "This is for you."

"You didn't need to buy me a present."

"I wanted to get you flowers, but the flower shop doesn't sell cut flowers." His brow wrinkles and he scratches his neck. "The owner, Eden I believe was her name, explained how cut flowers are destroying the earth. She asked me if I wanted to buy something else, but I left before I was forced to listen to another lecture. She was on the terrifying side."

"The people of Winter Falls take the environment seriously. It's why I don't have air conditioning in the inn. I couldn't get a dispensation."

"Boy does this town love its dispensations," he mutters.

I don't have a response, since he's not wrong, and peek in the bag at what he bought me instead. I have to cough to cover up my laugh when I realize what it is. "You went to *Sensual Scents*?"

"Women like candles."

"Did the owner explain to you what kind of candle this is?"

"There are different types of candles?"

"Petal's candles aren't 'normal' candles." I stop there. Do I tell him what kind of candle he bought?

"I'm officially intrigued. You need to explain."

"It's a sex candle," I blurt out and feel my face heat.

He doesn't blink as he stares at me. "A sex candle? Like to get you in the mood?"

I giggle. "Um, no. This particular candle is a wax play candle. Please don't ask me how I know. The story is not appropriate for a first date." Shit. I said date. Is this a date? Do I want it to be?

Cole doesn't notice my faux pas. "As in dripping candle wax?"

"Exactly. Petal also has massage candles. They're filled with essential oils and have aphrodisiac properties."

"She could be my grandmother," he whispers.

"Yep. And, if you let her, she'll talk your ear off about her sex life with her husband."

He gulps. "I think I'll avoid her shop from now on."

He's silly if he thinks he can steer clear of Petal by avoiding her shop. She's hardly there, which begs the question of how she manages to pay her rent. I asked. She has an online store. Nowadays, the brick and mortar shop is merely for show.

"If you're worried about old ladies filling you in on their sex lives, you'll want to avoid *Clove's Coffee Corner* as well. She's not as bad as Petal, but she does try."

"This town is odd," he murmurs and my stomach clenches.

What are you doing, Ellery? You know out-of-towners never stay and long-distance relationships don't work. It's fine. I'm not in love with Cole. I met him yesterday for goodness sake. I can have a bit of fun with the man without my heart getting trampled on. I'm no longer some naïve college kid.

I wiggle my eyebrows to cover how much his words hurt. "But fun. Am I right?"

I love Winter Falls. Are the people odd? You betcha. They're also super fun. And no one judges anyone else here. You want to run around without pants on? Go for it. But be prepared for everyone to know your business. Because as much as they don't judge, they do stick their noses where they don't belong.

The timer above the stove beeps, and I rush to the kitchen before the pasta can overcook. "I hope you like spaghetti."

"Who doesn't love spaghetti?"

I glance over my shoulder to wink at him. "Correct answer."

"What can I do to help?"

"You can get yourself a drink. There's wine on the table, but I have beer in the refrigerator if you prefer."

"Wine's fine," he says as he stirs the pasta sauce. He holds the spoon up to his nose and sniffs. "This smells delicious. Did you make it yourself?"

"My mom's the cook in the family. Not me. She makes up these huge batches of tomato sauce each year when tomatoes are in season. Lucky for me, she always gives me a few dozen jars."

I finish preparing the meal and we take our seats around my kitchen table. I always thought the table was perfect for two people, but I've never had a nearly six-foot-tall man sitting across from me before. Our legs press against each other. Maybe this table is perfect for two people after all.

"The garlic bread is delicious." Cole moans around a bite, and I wish he was biting something else. Namely, any part of me would be fine.

"It's my own creation. Don't ask me for the recipe, though. It's a secret."

"Let me guess. If you tell me, you'd have to kill me."

"Exactly." I wink.

I finish my wine and he reaches to fill my glass but stops with the bottle poised above my glass. "You have to work tomorrow. Are you sure you want a second glass?"

Uh oh. Red flag. "Are you trying to tell me how much I can drink?"

His eyes widen before he quickly refills my glass. "Of course, not. I just meant working with a hangover is a bitch."

"Good thing I don't get hangovers then, isn't it?"

He narrows his eyes on me. "You don't get hangovers?"

"Nope."

"Ever?"

"Never ever."

"I think I hate you."

"You can join the club. My sisters hate me, too. Although, their hangovers are their own fault. Mixing tequila shots with wine is a bad idea."

"How many sisters do you have?"

I groan. "Four."

"And having four sisters is bad?"

"I'll try and explain. My oldest sister, Aspen, has been in love with the Chief of Police forever. They were hot and heavy in high school, but then she took off for Dallas. She's been heartbroken for a decade, but she's too stubborn to realize he's heartbroken, too." Although with my sister now in town, things are going to change whether she wants them to or not.

"I'm the next oldest and, obviously, I'm perfect."

Cole inclines his head. "Naturally."

"Then comes Lilac. She's an environmental engineer who doesn't understand emotions." He chuckles. "I'm serious. She can't understand sarcasm. I'm fairly certain she was adopted."

"Wait. Lilac West is your sister?"

"According to Mom and Dad. Do you know her?"

"She's on the board to choose who wins the contract to build the community center."

Of course, she is. If it involves Winter Falls and the environment, Lilac has her hand in it.

"Uh oh. Are we being inappropriate by having dinner together? Are you using me to get to my sister? I hate to break it to you, but it won't work. You're welcome to try, though." I waggle my eyebrows. "I have suggestions for how you can try to influence me if you need a list."

His eyes heat. "I think I can figure out a few ideas on my own."

My belly warms and a delicious tingle spreads from my chest down my abdomen to my core. I bet he has a few ideas.

"But first I want to hear about the rest of your family."

My nose scrunches of its own accord. He does? In my experience, no one outside of Winter Falls wants to hear about my family. He reaches across the table and begins rubbing circles into my hand with his thumb.

"I like to know a woman before I take her to bed."

Oh boy. I shiver at the vision of him naked in my bed.

He smirks. "I'm glad we're on the same page."

I throw my rulebook – which clearly forbids me from getting involved with inn guests or out-of-towners – out of the window. My inhibitions aren't far behind it. I want this man and I haven't wanted a man in a long ass time. I haven't had a man in even longer. Screw it. I deserve to get what I want this one time.

"My page says we skip the rest of the getting to know you portion of the evening and proceed to the portion where we make use of the nearest bed." I wave my hand toward my bedroom. "I happen to know there's a perfectly good bed not more than twenty feet away."

He stands and pulls me to my feet before drawing me near. "It'd be a shame to let a perfectly good bed go to waste."

I shiver at how husky his voice has become. "A damn shame."

Chapter Five

Cole

I tighten my grip on Ellery's hand and rush to the bedroom. I can't believe this is happening. I'm not exactly a monk, but I don't usually jump into bed with a woman within days of meeting her either. I normally prefer to get to know someone before I add sex to the relationship. But when she suggested we skip the getting to know you portion of the evening, I couldn't say no.

I have wanted this woman since I first laid eyes upon her perfect heart-shaped ass. When she stood and I got a glimpse of the rest of her short, curvy body, I ached to pull her into my arms. I don't know what kind of magic she's using on me, but frankly, I don't care right now.

When we reach the bedroom, Ellery wrenches out of my hold and pushes past me.

"Sorry. I didn't plan…" Her laughter edges toward hysterical as she rushes around picking clothes up off the bed and from the floor.

"I promise I'm not one of those romance movie heroines who couldn't decide what to wear for her date," she says as she opens the closet doors and tosses the pile of clothes in her hands inside.

I'm relieved to see her flustered. Now I know this whole evening wasn't some type of practiced seduction on her part. I feel guilty for even thinking it could be. Ellery West is not a temptress. She's a small-town innkeeper. A sexy as hell innkeeper.

She slams the door to the closet shut, but it doesn't shut completely so she throws her body against the doors to get them to close.

I chuckle and she glares at me. "I'm not a slob."

I smirk. "And there wasn't a pile of dishes in your sink when I arrived either."

"You weren't supposed to notice." How could I not notice? They were piled higher than the faucet. I cock an eyebrow and she huffs. "Fine. You were supposed to pretend to not notice."

"Forget I said a word."

She rolls her eyes and steps away from the closet. A loud thud sounds from behind her, and she freezes. She waits for a few seconds but when no other sounds burst from the closet, she continues to me.

"Now. Where were we?"

She gazes up at me and bites her bottom lip, and I realize I haven't kissed those luscious lips yet. It's a mistake I'm correcting this second.

My hands cradle her cheeks, and she fists the front of my shirt before pushing up on her toes to meet me in the middle. Our lips collide. She doesn't hesitate before opening up for me. My tongue invades her mouth, and I'm lost. She tastes of strawberries, goodness, and the wine we drank for dinner, and I can't get enough.

Her hands release my shirt to wrap around me. She draws me near until I can feel her nipples rubbing against my chest. Two can play at this game. I thrust my hard length against her belly, and she lifts her leg to encircle my hips. It's not enough.

I squeeze her waist and lift her before taking two steps forward to lay her on the bed. She wrenches her mouth from mine.

"I thought you'd throw me on the bed," she gasps out between breaths.

"Next time," I tell her before trailing kisses down her neck to her chest. She's wearing a white blouse with tiny pearl buttons, and I can't want to open her up like my very own Christmas present.

Her hands tangle in my hair and she pushes my head toward her chest. "Is someone impatient?"

She wiggles beneath me. "It's been a while."

I freeze. "How long is a while?"

"I'm not some lily-white virgin. I went to college. But choices are limited in a town of a thousand people, most of whom you either knew when they were picking buggers out of their nose or who are old enough to be your grandparent."

"Good thing I'm not old enough to be your grandfather," I murmur as I undo the first two buttons of her blouse.

"I'm more relieved I didn't witness you picking your nose as a child. Gross."

The laughter freezes in my throat when I open her blouse to reveal the white lacy bra she's wearing. The lace does nothing to hide her pink nipples straining for freedom. I take a chance and bite down on one. She moans as her back arches nearly throwing me off of her.

I smile against her skin. Someone likes a hint of pain. Good to know. I pull the lace cups down until her breasts are revealed. I take a moment to admire the round globes of flesh before pinching her nipple. In response, she wraps her legs around my waist and rubs her center against my cock.

I push on her thighs. "No getting yourself off. It's what I'm here for."

She doesn't budge. "You're too slow."

I lean up on my elbows to study the picture below me. Her face is flushed, her eyes glazed over, and her blonde hair is spread across the pillow. The blush on her cheeks travels down her neck all the way to the tops of her breasts. I want to explore every single inch of her.

I maneuver until I'm kneeling above her. Her legs fall open and she grunts. "This doesn't feel like you speeding things up."

"We have all night."

"Except my alarm is set for five a.m."

My hands still. Five a.m.? The early alarm does limit our playtime. But playtime isn't over yet.

I unbutton the rest of her blouse until I can slide the material out of my way. She lifts up enough to remove the blouse completely. Bummer. I was enjoying how wanton she appeared with her blouse unbuttoned to show off her breasts. Before I have a chance to stop her, her bra is gone as well. Leaving her completely topless.

"Your turn."

I unsnap her jeans. "Oh, it's my turn all right." I lower the zipper and push the material down her legs. She kicks her legs to rid her of the material, leaving her in nothing but her panties.

I stroke my hands from her ankles along the smooth skin of her legs until I reach her panties. They're white lace and match the bra she was wearing. I'm relieved she isn't shaved smooth. Completely hairless may be the trend but it does nothing for me.

She wiggles. "Are you going to stare at me all night long or are you going to touch?"

My index finger glides up and down her slit over her panties and her breath hitches. "Stop rushing me."

"Stop being—" Her words cut off when I pinch her clit. She moans and thrusts her core in my hand.

Time to speed things up. I pull her panties down her legs until she's completely naked and laid out before me. Christmas came early this year. I reach for her core and use my fingers to open her up to me. She spreads her legs without any prompting.

"Good girl," I murmur against her skin.

I circle my tongue around her clit until her hands fist in my hair. I wait until her hands are tugging on the strands before latching onto the nub of nerves and sucking.

"Cole," she moans as she clenches my head to keep me where I am. She has nothing to worry about. I'm not going anywhere.

I tease her opening with my finger as I nibble and bite on her clit. My cock twitches when I feel her fingernails dig into my scalp. She's not the only one who enjoys a bit of pain. I thrust my finger into her, and she immediately clenches around it as she comes.

"Cole!" she gasps as she rides out her climax on my hand and mouth.

I wait until she collapses on the bed before I remove my finger and lift my head. She smiles down at me.

"Ready for round two?" I ask her.

"I don't know. Can you top round one?"

"I can try."

She motions for me to get on with it. I don't need any more prompting. My cock is already leaking and begging me to get this show on the road.

I whip my shirt off before shoving my jeans down my thighs releasing my cock. I come down over her and pin her hands above her head. I freeze poised at her opening. "Shit. Condom."

"Don't look at me. I don't keep condoms in my nightstand despite all the gazillion lessons from my mom."

Gazillion lessons from her mom? What is she— Never mind. Condom. I need a condom. I roll to the side and fish my wallet out of the back pocket of my jeans. I remove the condom hidden there. I have no idea how long it's been in my wallet, but I can't be bothered with expiration dates at the moment. Not when I have Ellery panting in want beneath me.

I roll the condom on my length before climbing atop her once again.

"I don't think I've ever seen a man ...." The words die on her lips when I plunge into her. I thrust until I'm fully seated and my balls slap against her skin. The feeling of her warm, wet walls squeezing me has me pausing before I come quicker than a teenage virgin.

She squeezes me again. "Move."

I shackle her wrists in one hand and place her hands on the headboard. Confining her wrists does nothing to stop her teasing. Her back arches allowing her to rub her breasts against my chest. I moan at the feel of her nipples scraping against my skin. The teasing continues when she circles my waist with her legs and squeezes.

The tingling in my spine increases.

"You're not helping things," I tell her between grit teeth.

"And you're still not moving."

My nostrils flare as I try to rein in my climax. "You asked for it," I say and glide out before slamming back into her again.

Her breath hitches. "Hell yeah, I did."

I thrust into her again and again until I find my rhythm. Ellery's hands escape my hold, and she clings to my shoulders as she lifts her hips to meet my thrusts.

"You need to come," I growl before sneaking my hand between us to reach her clit. I pinch it and her muscles clench on my cock.

"I'm ..." She doesn't finish her sentence before throwing her head back and moaning long and loud as she comes.

Finally. My thrusts become erratic as my climax hits, and I chant her name. "Ellie. Ellie. Ellie."

I collapse against her as I come down from my high. I try to roll off of her, but she wraps me up in her arms and legs to keep me where I am.

I kiss her hair. "I need to deal with the condom." And then we need to talk.

She motions toward a door. "Bathroom's in there."

I quickly rid myself of the condom and wash my hands, but by the time I return to the bedroom, she's out cold. I crawl into bed with her and cuddle her close to me before joining her in sleep.

Chapter Six

My alarm beeps, and I groan. Five a.m. normally comes too early, but it most definitely comes too early when there's an arm pinning me to a hard, warm body cuddled behind me in bed.

Cole nuzzles my neck before whispering, "Don't go," in my ear. His scratchy barely awake voice has me rubbing my butt against his already hard length.

Another alarm beeps. Alarms will go off every two minutes until I get out of bed. The snooze button is easy to hit, but a new alarm every two minutes? It forces me to get up and get going every dang time.

I groan. "I need to get to work."

"You work too hard."

I freeze at his words. It's nothing new. Everyone in my family thinks I work too hard. But they don't know how difficult it is to be the sole owner and operator of a business.

I peel his arm off of me and roll out of bed. "I need a shower."

I hurry into the bathroom before awkwardness can flow out of my mouth. Do I kick him out of my bed? My apartment? Or do I tell him to get up when he's ready? I have no clue. I don't specialize in mornings after. In fact, I don't usually do mornings after at all.

Things are much simpler if you keep it to sex and goodbye. I'm a big, fat liar. I've never done sex and goodbye either. I don't exactly have an advanced degree in sexual encounters. Last night was my first one-night stand.

When I open the door to my bedroom after a quick shower, I notice the bed is empty. My heart squeezes. Where did he go? Stop it, heart! Out-of-towner. We don't get involved with out-of-towners, remember? Fun and sexy times only!

I dress in my uniform of a white blouse and dark slacks. It's not actually a uniform, but the clothes feel like one since the moment I put them on I become 'Ellery the Innkeeper', and 'Ellery the Fun Person' disappears. Although, if I'm being honest with myself, Ellery the Fun Person hasn't made many appearances in the past years since I bought the old mansion to renovate it to make a bed and breakfast.

I walk into the living room and screech to a halt when I notice Cole at the stove in my kitchen.

"You're still here?" *Do I detect a hint of hope in your voice, Ellery?* Knock it off. You know better.

"I know you have food available at the inn, but I doubt you get much time to eat during the breakfast service." He's not wrong. "I thought I'd make you a breakfast sandwich."

"A breakfast sandwich?"

"An egg and sausage muffin, but way better than any fast food restaurant food."

I'll take him at his word as I haven't eaten at a fast food restaurant since I graduated from college over nine years ago.

"It smells good."

He removes the toast from the toaster and sets it on a napkin. "Listen," he tells the plate, "we should talk."

And here I thought I was maneuvering the whole morning after thing so well. "What about?"

He frowns at me. "Don't be coy." Before I have a chance to deny it, he continues, "I'm in town for another week. Then, I'm back in Chicago. If my firm gets the contract for the community center, I'll be in town quite a lot over the next two years. We can make this work."

Hold up. "Make what work?"

"Us. A relationship."

A relationship? "I don't do relationships."

He cocks an eyebrow. "At all?"

"Let me re-phrase, I don't do long-distance relationships." Although, truth be told, I haven't done many relationships either.

"And as I explained, I'll be in town often over the next two years."

He'd still be away more than here. He'd be free to do whatever the hell he wants when he's not here and I wouldn't be any the wiser. Been there. Done that. Have the scars to remind me of what an idiot I was. Not again.

"I don't think it's a good idea."

"Why?"

My mouth gapes open as I stare at him. I didn't expect him to question me. Most men are happy when you say you don't want a relationship. Or, at least, I assume they are. I don't have any actual experience to base my beliefs upon, but I read. And watch television.

"Because."

Great answer, Ellery. Way to be an adult and go after what you what. But what if what I want is standing in front of me appearing all sexy with his hair mussed up after a night of awesome sex? My core heats and my nipples tingle as I remember his hands all over my body last night. I'm down for a repeat but relationship? *Stay strong, Ellery.*

"Because why?"

Damn. While I was reliving the memories of last night, he moved until he's standing in front of me. Close enough I can feel the heat of his body. My hand lifts to touch his chest. He captures it and lays it across his heart.

"What are you afraid of, Ellie?"

"I'm not afraid."

He leans down and kisses the corner of my lips. "You can tell me," he whispers against my lips. His breath wafts against my face before he bites down on my earlobe.

I moan. I always did like a bit of teeth and biting with my sexy times. "Tell you what?"

His body shakes with his laughter. Grease sizzles in the pan and he hurries back to the stove to finish making breakfast. Without him in my immediate space, my brain reengages. This is why it's safer to not be in a relationship. My brain forgets how to work when I'm with a man.

"You're not leaving yet. Why don't we see how things go instead of making plans this second?" I suggest because, despite my brave words, the idea of him being in town and not near me would be impossible for me to handle.

"After all, I don't know you very well. Maybe you're one of those people who clap when a plane lands." I do an exaggerated shiver.

His eyes widen. "I wouldn't dare."

"Phew." I run the back of my hand over my brow.

My phone beeps with a message. "Shit," I swear after skimming it. "I need to get going. Soleil can't find the coffee filters."

Cole presses the breakfast sandwich in my hand. "You need to eat."

The smell of sausage hits me and my stomach rumbles. I bite into the sandwich and moan. What is it about the combination of cheese, egg, and sausage? Whatever it is, it's yummy.

I push up on my toes. "Thanks for the food," I say and kiss his cheek before rushing to the front door.

"We'll talk more tonight. It's my turn to cook."

He wants to cook for me? There's no time to evaluate why the thought makes my heart soar. I wave the sandwich at him. "And I'll let you."

I sprint down the stairs and across the parking lot to the backdoor of the inn. I don't stop running around until the clock strikes six. The inn is fully booked as this weekend is the Lammas festival. Twenty rooms may not seem like much, but when you're working with a skeleton staff since everyone in town is busy with the festival, twenty feels like a hundred.

I collapse in a chair in the kitchen and kick off my shoes. Bad idea. My feet are swollen. I probably won't be able to get them back on.

Someone knocks on the door, and I groan. It never ends. Even when everyone's checked in and had their complimentary beverage and extra towels, it doesn't end.

I force a smile on my face as the door opens. Cole peeks his head in.

"Hey! There you are," he declares as he enters and sits next to me.

"I'm glad it's you. I don't think I can deal with one more request for a synthetic foam pillow. There's a limit to the amount of times in a day I can have a conversation about synthetic versus natural materials."

"Tough day?"

"The worst. My feet are killing me."

He places my foot in his lap and begins rubbing it. When his thumb digs into my arch, I moan.

"Feels good."

He chuckles. "The moan kind of gave you away."

I narrow my eyes and shoot lasers at him, except I don't have the energy for shooting lasers and settle for a glare. Guessing by the grin on his face, I fail to appear stern.

My stomach rumbles. "I'm starving. I think I missed lunch."

"You think you missed lunch?" He tuts. "You need to eat to keep your energy up."

"Yes, Mom."

He tickles the bottom of my foot, and I yelp before snatching my foot back. "No tickling!"

We waggles his eyebrows. "You didn't seem to mind last night."

Because I was naked, and he was giving me the business. What was there to mind?

"I think you're going to have to carry me back to my place. I don't think my feet work anymore."

"About dinner..."

Here it comes. The brush off. I narrow my eyes on him. "What about it?"

"There's been an emergency with one of the architects back in Chicago."

This is not sounding good. "What kind of an emergency does an architect have? Did someone break a crayon?"

"You don't have a clue what being an architect entails, do you?"

I shrug. "Not really."

"I need to return to Chicago."

"Like now? This very minute?" I check the clock. It's quarter after six in the evening. You don't begin a road trip at night. At least, not in my limited experience.

"Unfortunately, yes. I want to get a few hours of driving in before I stop for the night as I promised to be in Chicago by the day after tomorrow."

"I guess dinner's off." My feet slap the floor as I stand. "Let me make you a sandwich for the road."

He captures my wrist and tugs until I end up sitting on his lap. He kisses my neck and I practically melt into him. "This isn't goodbye. I'll be back in town when my firm wins the bid."

"When they win the bid? Don't you mean if?"

"Nope." He tweaks my nose. "We're going to win it. I'm positive."

"Conceited much?" I tease, although I find his confidence more than a little attractive. Let's face it. There isn't much I don't find attractive about this man.

"Confident is not conceited."

I roll my eyes. "Whatever."

He nips at my lips, but before things can become interesting, he lifts me and sets me on my feet. "Wave me off?"

"Are you a sailor off to conquer the Nazis and I'm some poor woman left behind on the home front?"

"Exactly. I'm off to sea. You should probably give me a pair of panties to remember you by."

I smack him. "Ew. Gross."

He grasps my hand and leads me to the hallway where he stops to pick up his packed suitcase. I guess he wasn't kidding about getting on the road immediately. We're quiet as we walk out of the inn to his jeep.

He stows his luggage in the trunk before his hands circle my waist and he maneuvers me until I'm backed up against his vehicle with him looming over me.

"I'll miss you, Ellie."

His mouth slams down on mine, and I don't hesitate to open. His tongue invades and mine immediately rushes to greet his. While our tongues duel, I clutch his shirt and pull him close until our bodies are pressed against each other. All too soon he slows the kiss until he can pull away.

"I'll be in touch," he says as he opens the driver's door and settles in. I remain silent as he switches on the engine and drives away.

I stand there until his rear lights disappear in the distance. Once he's truly gone, I rub my chest at the ache blooming there. Dang it. My heart got involved after a mere two days. Stupid heart. This is why I don't get involved with out-of-towners. They always leave, and I never will.

Chapter Seven

I roll over in bed to encounter a cold and empty side. Dang. It's been four weeks since Cole left, and I still imagine him in my bed every single morning. I'm obsessed and I don't like it one bit.

I check the clock – four-thirty in the morning. Another sleepless night. Welp. I might as well get up and head to work. There's no sense lollygagging in bed where I'll spend my time dreaming about a man I can't have.

A man who messages me every day despite my refusal to respond. I'm cutting the heartstrings attached to him as quickly as I can. Too bad my heart doesn't agree. I rub my hand over my chest where it aches. It's heartburn, I tell myself. Not heartache.

"Hey, boss lady," Moon greets when I enter the inn thirty minutes later. "You're early."

"And you're entirely too bright-eyed and bushy-tailed considering you worked at the brewery until closing."

She winks. "Because I haven't gone to sleep yet."

"Please tell me you and my sister Ashlyn weren't causing trouble all night long."

Moon and my baby sister have been getting in trouble since the two of them were knee high. I wish I could blame Moon for all of their shenanigans, but I know my sister is the instigator nine times out of ten. Ashlyn is a troublemaker of the highest order.

"Okay. I won't tell you."

"Will I be getting a visit from Chief Alston?"

She giggles. "Don't be silly. Ashlyn and I have learned our lesson."

"I hope so," I mutter under my breath.

I survey the breakfast preparation. Things appear to be on schedule. The muffins and fresh bread have arrived from the bakery, *Bake me Happy*, the cheese and meat platters are ready, and the sausage is sizzling in the pan.

"What about omelets and scrambled eggs?" I open the fridge as I ask and my head rears back at the smell. "What the hell?"

"Sorry. One egg was rotten. I thought I got rid of the smell."

I slam the refrigerator close and take deep breaths as my stomach rolls. I place a hand on my middle to calm it, but nothing's helping. "I'm going to..."

I don't bother finishing my sentence before marching off to open the door. I take gulps of fresh air from outside until I'm convinced my stomach is going to keep down its meager contents.

"Sorry, boss lady," Moon apologizes again when I return.

I wave away her concern. She currently works as a waitress at the brewery in town, but her goal is to become a chef. I agreed to give her a chance despite her lack of qualifications. I know she's worried I'm going to fire her now, but it's not her fault one of the eggs was bad.

"I'll check with Phoenix later and ask if other customers complained about rotten eggs."

Phoenix is a dairy farmer who makes the best goat cheese in the world. He's also one of Lyric's brothers. Lyric's other brother, River, gives tourists green tours.

Lyric and my sister, Aspen, are trying to work things out since she finally knows the truth about the day she left town. I've never seen her happier. And I'm not jealous at all. Nope. I'm not. I don't need a man. And I certainly don't have time for one.

"Let me whip you up an omelet for breakfast," she offers.

"Mushrooms and—"

"Cheese." She rolls her eyes. "I know."

"I'll be in my office."

Office sounds way more glamorous than what the room actually is. It's a tiny area I carved out underneath the stairwell. There's enough space for a desk, a filing cabinet, and two chairs. Usually, I drag my computer into the kitchen to work, but with Moon preparing breakfast, I'll stick to my office.

I collapse in my chair. Insomnia is a bitch. I'm tired all the time, but I can't seem to fall asleep at night. I blame Cole. If it weren't for him, I wouldn't have all these sexy dreams and wake up feeling unfulfilled. Stupid man.

My phone beeps with a message. *Enough contemplating men, Ellery.* Time to work. Except the message isn't about work. It's Cole.

Good morning, Ellie.

I ignore the message the same way I've ignored his messages for the past four weeks. I told him I didn't want a relationship. When is he going to get the hint? Apparently not today since my phone beeps with another message from him.

You can't ignore me forever. Davis Williams will get the contract for the community center. And I will be coming back to town.

The temptation to convince Lilac to not award Cole's firm the contract is real. The problem is my sister will want a reason, and there's no way I'm telling her about Cole. She wouldn't understand my feelings since she's part robot. Plus, she doesn't believe in mixing work decisions and private life.

Ugh! I throw my phone into a drawer and slam it shut. If I can't turn the thing off, I can at least keep it out of my sight.

The door swings open and Moon sashays in carrying a plate with an omelet and a cup of coffee.

"Here you go," she says as she sets the items on my desk.

My stomach rumbles, and I lean over to sniff the food. One whiff of the omelet and my stomach switches from hungry to upset. I slam a hand over my mouth as I rush out of my office, shoving Moon to the side as I go. I barely make it to the powder room before I lose the contents of my stomach.

I kneel next to the toilet and inhale deep breaths until I'm certain my stomach is done playing explosive before rinsing my mouth with water and washing my hands. I open the door to discover Moon pacing the hallway.

"I'm sorry, Ellery. I swear I checked to make sure the eggs were fresh."

I pat her shoulder. "It's okay, Moon. But let's skip the eggs for breakfast this morning. Can you whip up some pancakes instead?"

"Of course. Sorry again." She rushes off.

I return to my office. I sigh when I note the omelet is missing. I gulp down half the cup of coffee before switching on my computer. Time to get some work done. First off, today's arrivals. I check the date and freeze.

No, it can't be. There is no way today is August 31st. *Shit. Shit. Shit.* I'm late for a very important date. I grab my phone and check my app, but I haven't miscalculated. My period is two weeks late.

I hear the creak of the stairs above the ceiling. Great. The first guests are on their way down for breakfast. I force thoughts of being late out of my mind and stand to help with the breakfast service.

Breakfast is a whirl of refilling coffee, taking pancake orders, and advising guests on the best things to do in Winter Falls. By the time Moon and I have fed all the guests and cleaned up the dining room, it's eleven o'clock.

I assess the kitchen area. It's clean and everything has been properly labeled and stored in the refrigerator or the pantry.

"You can go, Moon. I'll see you tomorrow."

Moon wrings her hands. "I really am sorry about the eggs."

I wave away her concern. I no longer think the eggs were the problem, but I can't tell her what I suspect the problem to be. No one in this town can keep a secret. Least of all my baby sister's best friend who thinks tattling to Ashlyn is a sport.

Once she's gone, I check to make sure the cleaner is on schedule before leaving the inn. I wave at everyone I encounter as I stride down Main Street toward *Nature Coop*, the general store. I don't stop to chat with anyone since I'm on a mission, but I know better than to ignore the town's gossips.

Failing to acknowledge the other residents of Winter Falls would cause them to run to the town's Facebook page to begin speculating on what's wrong with Ellery. The verdict's not in yet. But I'm afraid it starts with a P.

The second I enter *Nature Coop*, I realize my error. Feather, Petal, and Cayenne are standing at the check-out chatting with the owner, Shine. There is no way I can buy a pregnancy test without the entire town knowing about it before I exit the store. I whirl around to flee before they spot me.

"Ellery!"

Too late. I fish my phone out of my purse and put it to my ear. "Give me a second," I tell the phone before laying it against my chest and smiling at the ladies. "Sorry. This call is important."

"Ellery Promise West! I'm not deaf. I know your phone didn't ring," Feather accuses.

"It's on silent," I claim, but I feel my face heat with my lie.

Cayenne wags her finger at me. "Why are you lying?"

"I'm not—" Of freaking course, my phone rings and cuts me off proving I'm a liar. I read the screen. "It's the inn," I declare before rushing out of the store as fast as my short legs can move me.

The phone conversation doesn't last long. Does no one who works at the inn know where the coffee filters are besides me? When I hang up, I realize I'm at the courthouse where the town keeps a car available for residents who don't have a vehicle of their own for emergencies. Screw it. I'm declaring my situation an emergency.

As I drive out of town, I glance in my rearview mirror to check I'm not being followed. I sound paranoid. If you'd met the people in Winter Falls, you'd understand. I drive twenty miles past the closest town to another town to make certain I'm not spotted.

I rush into the drug store and practically run to the feminine hygiene aisle. There's no *practically* about it. I am running. I don't bother reading the labels, I grab five various tests and rush to the check-out. By the time I'm back in the car, I'm heaving for breath like I ran a marathon.

I break all the speed limits as I drive back to town until I hit the town border. Then, I slow down. Chief Lyric Alston may be in love with my sister, but it won't stop him from giving me a speeding ticket.

I park the car in the lot behind city hall. I scan the area, but I don't notice anyone. I exit the vehicle and stroll away from Main Street.

Once I'm out of view of the main drag, I break into a sprint and don't stop until I'm in my apartment with the door locked behind me.

I lean against the door for a moment to catch my breath. I hope no one saw me. The last thing I need is the entire town thinking I'm pregnant before I've had a chance to take a test.

Speaking of tests. I slip off my shoes and march to the bathroom. Time to get this over with. I pee on the stick, set the timer, and then sit on the floor to await the results.

Please be food poisoning. Please be food poisoning. The four words are on repeat for the entire three minutes I wait.

The alarm goes off and I peek at the test. Shit. I'm pregnant.

Chapter Eight

Present Day

I can hardly believe what I'm seeing. Eight weeks ago, my baby sister was pining away for Rowan. Ashlyn never made a secret of how much she wanted the former football player, but he fought his attraction to her as if he were down two touchdowns in the last quarter of the Super Bowl and wasn't ready to admit defeat. Now, they own a recording studio together he built for her, and he just proposed.

Tears well in my eyes. Stupid hormones. I need to get out of here before I'm blubbering like a lovesick fool. I'm not lovesick. I'm not! Do I miss Cole? Yes, but it's the sex I miss. Not his blue eyes sparkling down at me or his brown hair I love to make a mess of. Or the way he made me feel special and treated me as more than a workaholic. *Way to convince yourself the sex was meaningless, Ellery.*

With everyone admiring Ashlyn's new studio, it's time for me to make my escape. Before I can retreat a single step, Aspen latches onto my upper arm.

"Where do you think you're going?"

I force myself to roll my eyes. "Back to work. Where else would I be going?"

"I wouldn't know since you're obviously keeping a secret from me."

She sounds hurt, and I contemplate admitting my secret to her. Of all of my sisters, I'm closest to Aspen. We're only two years apart in age and shared a bedroom while growing up. Maybe I should tell her. It would be nice to have someone to confide in.

"What are we talking about?" Juniper asks as she sidles up to Aspen. Her gaze bounces back and forth between the two of us and her forehead scrunches. "What's wrong?'

"Nothing's wrong," I'm quick to say.

Aspen's face flashes with pain, and I feel like the biggest bitch in the history of mankind, which is saying a lot since I met Rowan's ex-wife. The woman wrote the book on bitch.

"I need to get back to the inn," I lie.

I've always been a bit of a workaholic, but I don't need to be at the inn nearly as much as I've claimed these past three months. But I can't be around my sisters and keep my pregnancy secret. They'd sniff out my problem in no time. I'm convinced Aspen was a bloodhound in a previous life.

"You do?" Aspen cocks a brow. "I happen to know every single one of your guests is here celebrating the grand opening of Ashlyn's new studio."

"What's with the name Bertie's anyway?" Juniper asks. "Is it some inside joke between the two of them? I hope he doesn't call her Bertie in bed. Yuck."

"I think it's a reference to Bertie Wooster from the P.G. Woodhouse stories," Lilac answers as she joins us.

Aspen's jaw falls open. The woman is a bookaholic of the highest order which makes owning the local bookstore the perfect career for her. "You know who P.G. Woodhouse is?"

Lilac frowns. "Naturally. Don't you remember the play *Jeeves and Wooster in Perfect Nonsense* Ashlyn was in when she was in college? We went to see it together."

Ashlyn went to drama school but instead of pursuing an acting career, she became an audiobook narrator. Thus, the recording studio.

Aspen snaps her fingers. "Of course. I forgot."

"Anyway, why are you standing here in the corner?" Lilac scans the room. "Shouldn't we be celebrating Ashlyn's engagement with her?"

Aspen snorts. "I think Ashlyn and Rowan want to celebrate their engagement alone." She gestures toward the emergency exit of the building where the two are currently sneaking off.

"I guess she forgives him for being an ass yesterday," I mumble. Rowan majorly screwed up yesterday. I don't know if I would have forgiven him as quickly.

"Duh. She's been in love with him forever. Naturally, she forgives him. It doesn't hurt he told her he loves her in front of the whole town before presenting her with a complete recording studio and proposing to her." Juniper sighs. "Some men know how to do romance."

Aspen smiles as her gaze locks on Lyric as he saunters into the building in his police uniform. "They certainly do."

While I've been busy trying to hide my pregnancy from my family, Aspen and Lyric hashed out their past issues and he proposed. If someone had told me a mere four months ago, Aspen and Ashlyn would be engaged to the men they've loved forever, I would have peed myself laughing.

I freeze when I notice who's behind Lyric. Shit. What is Cole doing here? I plaster myself to the wall and start slipping sideways toward the emergency exit. The place is packed. Maybe he won't notice me.

Aspen blocks my path. "Nope. You're not fleeing to hide at the inn until you tell us your secret."

"I don't hide at the inn."

"Tell it to someone who believes you."

"Are we referring to Ellery being pregnant?" Lilac asks.

While Juniper and Aspen gasp, I glare at Lilac. "How do you know?"

"It wasn't difficult to puzzle out. You haven't been drinking and you've been feeling nauseous a lot."

"I never said I was feeling nauseous."

Lilac sighs. "You don't have to say it for it to be true. It was obvious."

And here I thought I was hiding my condition from everyone.

"Can we not talk about this here?" I hiss. I don't want the entire town knowing. Not until I decide how I'm going to handle the situation.

Lilac studies me. "You won't be able to hide your pregnancy much longer. You'll begin showing soon."

Behind her, someone inhales sharply. I close my eyes and allow my head to fall back against the wall. This is not how I intended for him to find out.

"You're pregnant," Cole grumbles. "Is it mine?"

Before I can respond, my sisters are ushering me out of the building while Lyric herds Cole outside with us. They push us into the alley between the brewery and the recording studio.

"You don't have much time before the natives get restless," Lyric says before positioning himself at the mouth of the alley to guard our privacy.

I whirl on Cole. "How dare you ask if it's yours? Do you think I'm some kind of slut who sleeps with all her guests? If that's what you think, you can leave this minute."

He rubs a hand down his face. "I'm sorry. You shocked me. I don't think you're a slut." He pauses. "It's true? You're pregnant?"

I feel tears well in my eyes as I nod. "Yeah. I'm pregnant."

Cole's shock switches to anger. "And you didn't think to tell me?"

My hands ball into fists. How dare he? "I was going to tell you."

"When?" he exclaims. "When the kid graduates from college?"

"No," I hiss at him. "When I've made a decision about what to do."

His eyes widen, and he retreats a step. "Do you not want my baby?"

His baby? I'm pretty sure it's more mine than his at the moment. "I want him to grow up with a family, not a single mom."

"It's a boy?"

"Impossible," Lilac says from the end of the alley where she's obviously been listening. "According to my calculations, Ellery is not yet eighteen weeks, which is when it's possible to ascertain the gender."

Cole's eyes narrow and I can tell he's counting. "Eighteen weeks sounds about right. It's a boy?"

"I don't know. I haven't had my mid-pregnancy ultrasound yet." But I think of the baby I'm growing as a boy who resembles Cole with his curly brown hair and blue eyes.

"I like the idea of having a girl. A girl with your green eyes and your nose."

I cover my nose with my hand. "My nose? What's wrong with my nose?"

He grasps my hand and pulls it away from my face before kissing the tip of my nose. "It's adorable."

I bite my lip as I stare up at him. His eyes are full of warmth and doubts creep in as to why I've been pushing him away. Am I stupid? This gorgeous man is gazing at me as if he cares for me. Not like he's been carousing around with who knows what type of hussies back in Chicago.

"Guys. You can get all lovey-dovey later. For now, we need to get you two out of here," Lyric announces as he marches toward us. "I'll escort Cole back to the inn. You join the party with your sisters."

Aspen shackles my wrist. "Thanks, babe."

Lyric kisses her forehead before leaving with Cole.

"Back to the party," I say and yank on my wrist.

Aspen snorts. "You're daft if you think we're returning to the party when we just found out you're pregnant."

"And by a hot guy!" Juniper fans her face. "Where have you been hiding him?"

Lilac raises her hand. "I know who he is."

And I need to get the hell out of here before she spills all my secrets. I yank harder on the wrist Aspen has shackled but she tightens her hold.

"Well," Aspen presses, "who he is?"

"He's an architect. His firm bid on the community center project," I explain.

"What's the deal?" Juniper asks. "Have you been having an affair with him for months?" Her nose scrunches. "No. You can't have been. He'd know you were pregnant. Unless it's a long-distance relationship."

Aspen snorts. "A long-distance relationship? Ellery? No way."

"Careful," I hiss at her. She promised to keep the reason for my aversion to long-distance relationships secret.

She frowns. "You shouldn't keep secrets from your sisters."

I spit daggers out of my eyes at her. She's one to talk. She kept the reason she wouldn't forgive Lyric a secret for a decade. "Pot meet kettle."

"It's not the same thing," she huffs.

Juniper forces her way in between us. "Can you speak slowly for the rest of the class, please?"

"I must say even I'm lost," Lilac says.

My phone rings. Praise the heavens!

"Go ahead." Aspen releases my wrist. "Run away. But this conversation is not over." She stomps off.

"Not over," Juniper repeats as she follows Aspen.

"We'll discuss this later," Lilac says, because she wouldn't know how to make a threat even if it is to her sibling.

As I watch them stalk away, I start planning how I can avoid them for the next eighteen to twenty-two weeks. No, not weeks. Make that years. Maybe I can find an exchange program for innkeepers.

Chapter Nine

Cole

Lyric escorts me to his golf cart. I'm surprised since the bed and breakfast is mere doors down the street, and everyone in this town prefers to walk whenever they can.

"Hop in," he says before fishing out his phone. He puts it on speaker before he dials. "Meet me at the falls," he says when the phone connects.

"Dude, this better be important. I'm celebrating my engagement with the woman I love," the voice on the other end of the phone grumbles.

"Ellery's pregnant, and I'm with the baby daddy."

Holy crap. Ellie's pregnant. I didn't see that coming. Is the pregnancy why she's been avoiding my phone calls and not returning my texts? Is she afraid I'll run the other way? Not happening. I would never abandon my child.

"Does Ashlyn know?"

Ashlyn as in Ellie's younger sister? Who is this guy and why did Lyric phone him? I need to get out of here before things get any weirder than they already are.

"I can ..." I wave toward the inn.

Lyric shakes his head and points to the golf cart. "Get in."

Despite having a hunch this has nothing to do with his position as the chief of police, I don't dare ignore a police officer.

"Meet you in five," Lyric says and ends the phone call.

"What's going on?" I ask as he jumps into the golf cart.

He grunts in response.

"Am I in trouble?"

He snorts.

"Can you speak in actual sentences instead of sounds?" I know I'm pushing it. Winter Falls may be a tiny town in nowhere Colorado, but this man is the Chief of Police regardless of the size of the town.

"I'll explain when we get there."

"Where's there?" He's not taking me out into the field to shoot me, is he? I've read those Lee Child books. I know cops in small towns aren't always on the up and up.

"The falls."

The falls? As in the waterfall the town is named after? Ellie told me it's beautiful at the falls, but I didn't have a chance to visit the last time I was in town since I had to return to Chicago earlier than I expected.

Less than five minutes later, Lyric pulls the golf cart to a stop at the top of a waterfall. Wow. It is gorgeous. Even though it's December and most of the trees are barren, the nature remains impressive.

"Follow me," Lyric orders as he strides toward an open field.

Another golf cart pulls up and I wait as a man climbs out and marches toward me.

My eyes widen when I recognize him. "Holy shit. You're Rowan Hansley." Rowan Hansley was one of the best quarterbacks in the NFL before an illegal tackle ruined his knee.

He extends his hand. "And you are?"

"Cole Hawkins."

"Ellery's baby daddy." Lyric's words are like a slap to the face and effectively put an end to my fanning over the former football player.

Rowan squeezes my hand until the bones creak. Shit. He hasn't lost any of his legendary strength.

Lyric shoulders his way between us. "Don't kill him yet."

Rowan drops my hand and I grit my teeth to stop myself from massaging the pain. I'll be damned if I'll show any weakness in front of these two men. They may be practical strangers to me, but they're connected to Ellie.

"You can't kill me. People know I'm in Winter Falls. They'll come searching for me."

Lyric and Rowan stand side by side and cross their arms over their chests while they glare down at me. I'm not short by any means at five-foot-eleven, but these men tower over me. They don't appear as if they care if people come after me. I try a different tactic.

"Do you want Ellie's child to grow up without a father?"

"The way I heard it, Ellie's not sure she's going to raise the child herself."

His words are a punch in the gut. I suck in air, but I can't breathe. Lyric clasps my neck and presses until my head is between my knees.

"Breathe. We can't have you dying on us out here."

I suck in air. "Then, you're not going to kill me for defiling Ellie?"

Rowan barks out a laugh. "Defiling? Have you not spent any time in Winter Falls? Once the town hears you got her pregnant, they'll cheer for you."

"After Mrs. West gives him a lecture about prophylactics," Lyric adds.

"I swear I used a condom."

Lyric nods. "Good. Use the same emphasis when you speak to Mrs. West and maybe Mr. West won't get out the shotgun."

I gulp. "The shotgun?" Are shotgun weddings a real thing? Or is Ellie's father going to murder me? "I need to sit down."

I stumble my way to a boulder and collapse on it. I bury my face in my hands. "I didn't think about Ellie's parents' reaction. I'm not ready to die. If the firm wins the bid for the community center, I'll make partner. I can't die before I make partner. And I want to watch my kid grow up. My kid. I'm going to be a dad."

"He's babbling," Rowan murmurs.

"I got this," Lyric says.

Whoosh! A bucket of water rains down over me.

I jump to my feet. "Fucking hell. The water is freezing."

"And now you know why the falls are named Winter Falls," Lyric says as he calmly returns the bucket to his golf cart as if he didn't just try to drown me. He pulls a blanket out of his kit and throws it at me. "Here. Can't have you dying of hypothermia."

I wrap the blanket around me before my teeth can start to chatter. "Can you stop the torture and kill me already?"

"We didn't bring you out here to kill you," Rowan claims.

"Half the town saw me drive off with you. If I kill you, it'll be when there are no witnesses."

Is he serious? I hope not. I play it off as a joke. "Good to know, Chief."

He slaps my back. "Call me Lyric since we're practically related now."

"You're with Ellie's sister Aspen?" He nods. "I thought you hated her."

He hooks his thumbs in his belt and leans back on his heels. "You've been gone a while. Aspen and I are engaged."

"And you're engaged to Ashlyn?" I ask Rowan.

He smiles. "Just asked her."

Great. We'll all caught up. "Can we stop the riddles now and you tell me why you brought me out here and tried to drown me?"

Lyric smirks. "Trust me. There won't be any trying if I decide to drown you."

Rowan chuckles. "Stop scaring the poor man. I imagine hearing you made your one-night stand pregnant is enough fright for a day."

I growl. "Ellie's not a one-night stand."

Lyric rubs his hands together. "Now we're getting somewhere."

"If you wanted to know about my relationship with Ellie, why didn't you just ask me?"

He smirks. "Where's the fun in asking?"

"At least someone's having fun," I mumble.

Rowan raises his hand. "Two someones are having fun."

"Is this how it's going to be from now on? You two ganging up on me?"

"I imagine whenever Juniper and Lilac find men, you'll gang up on them with us."

Rowan chuckles. "Can you imagine Juniper with a man? The woman loves animals more than humans."

"She has more of a chance than Lilac. I'm not certain Lilac's actually human."

"You're presuming I'll be around in the future," I interrupt to say.

Lyric cocks an eyebrow. "You won't? Your child will be in Winter Falls."

"Will he? Ellie said she wants the baby to have a family and not be raised by a single mother."

Rowan pats my shoulder. "Then, make sure Ellery knows you have her back."

"You do have her back," Lyric growls.

I nod. "Of course, I do." I want to have more than Ellery's back, but she ghosted me for the past months. I don't know where I stand with her.

Lyric prowls toward me with Rowan at his back. "You do? You're not merely saying you do because it would be easy for us to throw you over the falls and say you slipped?"

"You're not some dumb country bumpkin." The words slip out before I can stop them.

He crosses his arms over his chest. "And you didn't answer my question."

"I would never abandon my child. Never," I swear.

It's the truth. I refuse to be my father who thought it was perfectly normal to abandon his wife and child without so much as a goodbye. His genes may course through my body, but I am not him. I will never be him.

"You believe him?" Lyric asks Rowan.

Rowan tilts his head as he studies me. "I do."

"You're not just saying you do because he thinks you're a football god?"

"Hey! I never said he was a football god. I'm not a rabid fan who stalks players on social media and shows up at their house with presents."

Rowan grins. "He's obviously thought about it, though."

Lyric slaps his shoulder. "Come on. We need to get back. I have a fiancé who's probably losing her mind over her sister not telling her she's pregnant."

"And I have a fiancé waiting in my bed."

"Shut it. You're talking about my little sister."

Rowan winks. "But she's not my little sister." He climbs into his golf cart and waves as he drives off.

"Let's go. I'll drive you back to the inn."

Finally. I don't know exactly what happened, but it feels as if I passed some kind of exam except, I don't know what the test was for.

Chapter Ten

I startle awake at the sound of something clattering to the floor. My eyes scan the room as I try to figure out where I am. I notice the snow on the television and realize I'm laying on the couch. I guess I fell asleep here. Nothing new.

"Where is she?" Ashlyn asks from my bedroom. And now I know what clattered to the floor. It wasn't a what. It was a who.

"Keep it down," Aspen responds.

"Why? We're breaking into her house. She's going to figure out it's us eventually."

"Where are Juniper and Lilac?" I holler toward my bedroom.

"Present!" Juniper yells.

"I'm here also," Lilac says as she enters the living room while wiping imaginary dirt off of her pants.

"How did you get in here?" I made sure to lock all the windows and doors when I came home since I knew a sister invasion was bound to happen after they learned I'm pregnant.

"Don't insult us," Aspen says.

"I'm on the second floor."

"What's your point?" Ashlyn asks.

"Never mind," I mutter.

Aspen lifts my feet to sit on the sofa next to me while Ashlyn and Juniper sit on the floor in front of the television. Lilac drags a kitchen chair into the room.

"Oh good. We're all here."

"Yes." Lilac nods. "It's best we discuss things as a group."

"I was being sarcastic," I tell her.

"It doesn't change the accuracy of your statement."

"Have you talked to Mom?" Aspen asks, and I cringe. The last thing I want to do is tell my mom – the world's biggest advocate for safe sex in the entire world – about how I got pregnant by mistake.

"She won't be mad," Ashlyn claims.

"No, she'll be disappointed, which is ..."

"Worse!" my sisters shout in unison.

"Who is Cole and why haven't we heard of him?" Ashlyn taps her chin, and I notice her engagement ring sparkle.

"Shit, Ashlyn. I don't mean to steal your thunder. You got engaged today, and I haven't congratulated you yet."

She waves her ring at me. "No need to apologize. I got the guy in the end. It's all I ever needed." Her smile stretches from ear to ear.

"I'm happy for you." My eyes itch and I sniff before the tears can fall. "Damn pregnancy hormones."

"Don't blame the pregnancy. I cried for Rowan when he proposed, too," Juniper teases and Ashlyn shoves her over while she giggles.

"According to my information, Cole was only in town for a few days," Lilac says.

Of course, she knows how long he was in town. In addition to being a walking, talking encyclopedia, she doesn't forget anything. It's incredibly annoying normally, but more so when you grow up with her and think you've managed to get away with 'borrowing' her skirt 'for good'.

"You had a one-night stand." Ashlyn rubs her hands in anticipation. "Tell us all about it."

Juniper slaps her. "She didn't say she had a one-night stand. I still say the two of them could be in a long-distance relationship."

"Not a long-distance relationship," I mumble.

"Because of Bob." Aspen surmises. Correctly.

Lilac frowns at me. "What does your vibrator have to do with your views on long-distance relationships?"

"Not B-O-B. Bob. As in the name of a man," Aspen explains. I throw a glare her way. Who does she think she is? Telling all my secrets.

"Who's Bob and why don't we know about him?" Ashlyn sounds hurt.

Sigh. There's no way to tell this story without everyone getting their feelings hurt, which is why I didn't want to tell anyone. Time to come clean once and for all.

"I met Bob when I was a junior in college."

Ashlyn wrinkles her nose. "Can we pretend his name is Rodrigo or Diego? Bob sounds boring."

"Robert is a perfectly acceptable name. Although it's fallen in popularity, it remains the 80th most popular name for boys."

I glare at Lilac, the statistics machine.

"What? Why are you glaring at me? I'm merely stating facts."

"Can we get back to the story now, please?" Juniper pleads.

"Anyway, my entire junior year we were together and then Bob graduated. I loved him and didn't want to lose him, so we agreed to try long-distance." I hug a pillow to my stomach. "During my senior year, we kept in touch regularly and saw each other at least one weekend a month. I thought things were good. I even made plans to follow him to Seattle where he was working in the tech industry."

Ashlyn gasps. "You were planning to live somewhere other than Winter Falls for good?"

Aspen wraps an arm around my shoulders and squeezes me. "There's nothing wrong with leaving Winter Falls."

I don't respond to Ashlyn. I need to get this story out before I become a blubbering mess. I've been a blubbering mess entirely too much recently.

"I landed an interview for a big hotel in Seattle, but I didn't tell Bob. I wanted to make sure I had the job first. I flew out there and they offered me the job on the spot. I rushed to Bob's apartment to surprise him with my plans, except his surprise was bigger." I blink as fast as I can and wave my hands in front of my face as if the action will stop the tears from falling.

"She walked in on Bob with another woman. And not some scamp he pulled off the street either. His live-in girlfriend," Aspen finishes for me.

"What an asshole!" Ashlyn roars. "Let's go burn his house down."

"Must you always be dramatic? I can let Slinky lose in his place. Highly effective and no one has to know we were behind it."

I'm almost afraid to ask Juniper who or what slinky is. "Slinky?"

"Her pet snake." Ashlyn shudders. "And now you know why I no longer visit Juniper's house."

"I can send him a virus in an email. It will erase all the information on his phone and computer," Lilac suggests.

I slash my hands in the air in front of me. "No. No. No. We're not doing some big revenge thing against my ex. He's not worth it."

Aspen purses her lips. "Except what he did to you has made you afraid of relationships."

I bristle. "I'm not afraid of relationships."

"Then, why have you been ignoring Cole's calls and messages?"

I glare at Lilac. "How do you know he's been calling?"

She smirks. "Because you just confirmed it." She clears her throat before admitting. "And I may have done a bit of hacking."

"You can hack?" Ashlyn screeches. "Since when? Why haven't you offered your services to us before?"

Lilac's nose wrinkles. "Because I wouldn't do well in prison. You wouldn't either."

"Ha! I've never had a problem in jail before."

"What? When were you in jail?" Juniper asks Ashlyn.

Ashlyn's eyes widen. "Oops!"

Aspen claps her hands. "Let's return to the matter at hand. Besides, you can't possibly be surprised Ashlyn has been in jail before. You spent a night in jail with her, remember?"

"I want to know more about Ashlyn's criminal past," I insist.

Aspen wags a finger at me. "Liar. You're avoiding the subject. You don't want us to discuss how you're afraid to give Cole a chance."

"He's the father of your child. You can't ignore him forever," Lilac points out.

My hand automatically moves to my stomach. "Thanks for the reminder."

"Why didn't you tell us you were pregnant?" Juniper's voice is filled with hurt. I close my eyes and let my head fall back against the cushions.

"I was trying to ignore the situation," I admit.

Lilac coughs. "You can't ignore it for much longer. You're nearly mid-pregnancy. If you want to give the baby up for adoption, you need to—"

Ashlyn gasps. "Give the baby up for adoption? What?"

"She said she isn't sure what she wants to do," Juniper explains before I have a chance to respond.

"I'll take her." My eyes fly open to find Ashlyn staring at me. "Rowan and I will raise her until you're ready to handle being a mom."

"Did I enter an alternate universe? How is it possible my little sister is more responsible than me?"

"I think you mean parallel universe."

"I'm begging you," I plead. "Someone stop Lilac before she explains what a parallel universe is."

"Your aversion to science is going to catch up to you someday. I hope your child is a scientific wunderkind."

"I haven't even had the child yet and my sisters are arguing about who will raise her and whether she'll love science," I mutter to myself. "And you wonder why I didn't tell any of you about my pregnancy."

Aspen laughs. "You didn't tell us because you're terrified to have a relationship with your baby daddy."

Damn. Having a sister who knows your every secret and fear sucks sometimes.

"Cole isn't here to stay. He's not from here."

"And you're hiding behind where he lives in order to avoid having a relationship with the man. Try again." Aspen should have gone into psychotherapy instead of owning a bookstore.

"Cole being the father of my child doesn't mean I want to be in a relationship with him."

"Ha!" Aspen barks. "You don't have sex with men you don't like. You like him, but you're scared."

I throw my pillow at her. "Stop saying I'm scared."

"If the shoe fits," she sings.

I yawn and Lilac stands. "We need to let Ellery get some rest. Sufficient sleep is important during pregnancy."

I latch onto Lilac the fact pusher's statement and yawn again. "I am quite tired, and my alarm goes off at 5 a.m."

Ashlyn sighs. "You need to trust Moon to handle the breakfast service on her own."

"You're not exactly impartial since Moon's your best friend."

She sticks her tongue out at me. "I would never lie about food."

Aspen herds everyone out the front door. "Let's go. Baby mamma needs her rest."

I groan. "You better not refer to me as baby mamma for the next five months."

I slam the door and lock it before making my way to my bedroom to shut the window they crawled through. I know I should probably consider their advice, but I wasn't lying about how tired I am. Revealing secrets is exhausting. I'll worry about Cole and the baby tomorrow.

I rub a hand over my belly. Don't worry, baby. I'll figure it out before you arrive. I hope.

Chapter Eleven

"Have you seen Ellie?"

I freeze when I hear Cole ask Moon where I am. Shit. Where can I hide? My tiny office doesn't exactly have a wardrobe I can use to travel to another dimension. Where is Aslan, the King of Narnia, when you need him? I eye the area under the desk. It'll have to do.

I drop to my knees and scamper under the piece of furniture. Dang. The opening is even smaller than I thought. I'm pulling my chair in when the door opens.

"Huh," I hear Moon say. "I swear she was in here a second ago. Maybe she went to the bathroom?"

"It's fine. I'll wait here."

"It's your funeral," Moon sings as she shuts the door behind her.

The chair across from my desk scrapes as Cole pulls it out and sits in it. Crap. I don't have time to be trapped under my desk during the breakfast service. Why didn't I at least grab my phone before I snuck under here?

Cole whistles as if he has all the time in the world. Shouldn't he be asleep now? It's barely six in the morning. Who in their right mind is awake now except for me and Moon?

I wiggle to get more comfortable since I'm apparently stuck here for the foreseeable future. I still when my shoes squeak on the floor.

"You might as well come out from under there, Ellie."

I keep my mouth clamped shut. He can't possibly know I'm here.

"I can hear the wheels turning in your head."

Wheels don't actually turn in your head, according to Lilac.

"I can sit here all day. Can your bladder handle hiding under a desk for hours upon hours; needing to pee and not getting any relief?"

Asshole. My bladder has shrunk to the size of a pea since I've been pregnant.

"What gave me away?"

He kneels and peeks under the desk to face me. "Do you need help?"

He smiles and a dimple pops out on his right cheek. Not fair! I want to stick my tongue in the tiny indentation. He's also clean shaven and his blue eyes are sparkling. My inner hussy sighs before urging me to jump him. We did that and look what happened.

"I'm fine." My voice breaks. I clear my throat and try again. "I'm fine."

I crawl out from under the desk, and he extends his hands to help me up. I glare at his big, strong hands for a moment as I remember how they felt roaming my body. I shiver before pushing those sexy thoughts out of my mind.

Out of towner, Ellery. He won't stay. And you know what happens when the cat is away.

I grasp his hand and he uses the hold to pull me to my feet and into his body. I gaze up at him and his eyes flare. The attraction is mutual. Of course, it is. There's a reason I'm pregnant with his baby after all. Although, we only had sex the one time and he used a condom. Hold up. He used a condom and I got pregnant? One plus one shouldn't equal baby.

I slap his shoulders. "Did you stealth me?"

He doesn't budge. "What are you talking about?"

I slap him again. "Don't act stupid. When a man removes the condom during sex. Not okay, Cole. Not okay."

Now, he steps away to run a hand through his hair. "I didn't remove the condom. I would never. I am sorry, though. I didn't check the expiration date. I should have. I was a bit preoccupied."

I slam my fists on my hips. "Don't you dare blame me."

He holds up his palms as he slowly steps back until he's on the other side of the desk where he collapses in the chair. "I'm not. I'm sorry. I should have handled you with care. I didn't. Please accept my apology."

Crap. Why does he have to sound sincere? How can I hold onto my anger when he apologizes?

"It's fine. It takes two to tangle." He wiggles his eyebrows, but before he can speak, I continue. "Now, what can I do for you? Do you need some extra towels? A new pillow?"

"Why have you been avoiding me since my return to town?"

So much for my evasive maneuvering. I huff. "I haven't been avoiding you." Lie. "I've been busy."

"You hid from me under your desk because you're busy?"

Dang it. Can't he at least pretend he didn't discover me hiding? I'm having a child for goodness sake. I'm supposed to be the adult here.

"I was searching for a pen?"

"You can't avoid me forever."

Ha! I can try. I kept my pregnancy secret for four months in Winter Falls – the town where gossiping is considered an elite sport – I think I can do pretty much anything I put my mind to.

"We need to talk," he insists.

I'm not ready to talk. I have no idea what to do about the baby. Have it, obviously, but what about afterwards? Do I give him up for adoption? Do I raise him on my own? Do I let Cole be a part of the baby's life? How do I share custody with Cole and not get my heart broken?

"You only found out about the baby a few days ago. Maybe you should take some time to come to terms with his existence and then we'll talk."

"I've come to terms."

He has? How? I haven't come to terms yet and I've known about the baby for months now. "Yeah, sure."

"I'm serious. After Lyric and Rowan kidnapped me—"

"They did what?" I screech. "How dare they? You leave them to me. I'll handle them."

He smirks, and I realize I showed him my hand. Ugh! He's not supposed to know I care about him. I'm supposed to be the ice lady over here.

"What I meant to say is it's not okay for my brothers-in-law to kidnap people especially since Lyric is the Chief of Police."

Cole grins and it's obvious I'm not fooling him.

"They didn't harm me, except for the ice cold bath."

There's only one place to get an ice cold bath in town. I grab onto the topic change with both hands. "What did you think of the falls?"

"They're beautiful. I can't wait to see the area when the trees are full of leaves and the flowers are blooming."

What is he talking about? It's nearly winter. Blooming flowers are months away. "You won't be around then."

"I told you my firm is going to win the contract to build the community center and I'll be in town on a regular basis."

I sigh. "It doesn't matter. You'll leave afterwards and then—"

His growl cuts me off. "Don't you dare. Don't you dare say I won't be around for our child. I will always be there for her whether or not I'm in Winter Falls. You don't know me."

I latch onto his last sentence. Because I am not talking about him being there for our child. And it's not because the idea scares the pants off of me. "Exactly! I don't know you. I have no idea what kind of person you are. Maybe you're a horrible man who shouldn't be anywhere near our son."

And maybe I'm a big, fat liar who's going straight to hell in a handbasket.

"Good idea. Let's get to know each other."

I rear back. Did he seriously suggest we date? "As in date? Don't you think it's a little late to date when I'm carrying your baby?"

"Date. Hang out. We don't need to label it."

And give my heart a chance to latch onto him again? No way. *Too late, my heart whispers.* I ignore the whisper. My heart is confusing mind numbing good sex with feelings. *No, I'm not.*

"It's not a good idea. And it's unnecessary."

His eyes narrow on me. "Why isn't it a good idea? What are you afraid of?"

I bristle. Will everyone please stop saying I'm a scaredy-cat? "I'm not afraid."

"Excellent." He stands. "I'll pick you up for dinner at six."

I growl. "I said no. And if you're the man who you claim to be, you'll accept my answer."

He pauses with his hand on the doorknob. "Are you sure? I hear the burger at the brewery is excellent."

I retreat into my innkeeper persona. "It is. I'm happy to make a reservation for you."

"The town's announcing the winning bid tomorrow. Once you realize I'm here to stay, you'll change your mind. I can't wait to get to know everything about you, Ellie," he says as if it's a foregone conclusion before opening the door and striding away.

"What then?" I ask my now empty office. "What happens when the community center is built? You'll go away and forget all about me and your baby."

"Did you say something?" Moon asks as she pokes her head in my office.

"Nope." I stand. "Let's get the breakfast service going."

Work is what I need to get my mind off my troubles. I feel a flutter in my stomach. Don't worry, baby, I'll protect you. I won't let you down. I will never let you down. And I won't let anyone else let you down either.

Chapter Twelve

Cole

I study the room and note the entire town seems to have shown up for the announcement of who won the bid to design and build the community center. I sniff. Am I smelling popcorn? I glance behind me and find all of Ellery's sisters are here. They're drinking beer and eating popcorn.

"I'm Ashlyn." The blonde waves at me. "I'm Ellery's favorite sister."

"Are not. I'm Juniper, and I'm the favorite." Juniper bumps her shoulder, and then they shout in unison, "Drink!"

"Are you supposed to be drinking at a town meeting?"

Ashlyn points to the rear wall. "There's a bar."

Sure enough. There's a makeshift bar set up and it's doing good business judging by the line.

"It's completely legal. I don't know if you remember me. I'm Lilac." As if I could forget the woman in charge of evaluating the bids. "And this is Aspen."

Aspen waves. "I'm the oldest West sister."

Ashlyn rolls her eyes. "I'm the youngest. Mom stopped having babies after me because she obviously had achieved perfection with me."

"Behave, dream girl," Rowan growls as he sits next to me.

"But you enjoy it when I misbehave," she says with a waggle of her eyebrows.

"Does he punish you? Does he tie you up and spank you?" Juniper asks.

"Spanking is the most popular bondage activity," Lilac announces, and I choke on my water.

Rowan slaps my back harder than necessary. "You get used to them."

Lyric collapses in the chair on the other side of me. "Made it."

Ashlyn slow claps. "Good job, Chief. You managed to walk from your office to this room, which is in the same building."

"Careful," he growls at her. "Being my future sister-in-law doesn't mean you're above the law."

"I don't know what you mean." She flutters her eyelashes and even I can tell she's guilty as hell.

"I want my key back."

Aspen leans forward and smirks at him while holding out a key. "Ellery says hi."

Ellery? Where is she? I searched the room when I arrived, but I didn't notice her. I assume she's still hiding from me.

Rowan holds his phone out to me. I glance down at the display to see a picture of Lyric crawling out of a window. It's not the most flattering of pictures with his ass hanging out of the window. I cover my laugh with my hand. There's no need to anger the Chief of Police.

Lyric snatches the phone from Rowan and stands. "Who took this picture?" He holds up the phone and glares around the room.

"Wasn't me, Chief," a woman hollers.

Rowan leans close to whisper, "That's Sage. She's the police dispatcher and she definitely took the picture."

Sage speaks before I have the chance to tell him I met her the last time I was in Winter Falls.

"You can't fire me for taking a picture of you and posting it on social media," she claims.

"It's a violation of my privacy." Everyone laughs at Lyric's statement, including Rowan. Lyric glares at him.

"Did you forget you live in Winter Falls?" Rowan asks between bouts of laughter.

Lyric marches toward Sage who giggles before running away.

"What just happened?" I ask the room.

"We schooled you on what happens when you piss off a West sister," Ashlyn answers. "You've been warned."

"I should have checked the expiration date on the condom," I mumble.

"It might not have mattered," Lilac says. "The World Health Organization claims condoms have a two-percent failure rate, but the actual failure rate is closer to fifteen percent."

Ashlyn claps. "Thank you, Ms. Encyclopedia."

"I, for one, can't wait to meet mini Ellery. I hope it's a girl. I've already picked out a ton of cute pink outfits," Aspen says.

"And I have the perfect puppy picked out for her or him, I'm not fussy," Juniper adds.

"I'm designing a nursery in our spare bedroom so my little niece can stay over."

"I think we should have our own baby who can use the nursery," Rowan responds to Ashlyn who wags her engagement ring at him.

"Dude, no babies before marriage."

"Why not?" A middle-aged woman asks from behind me. When I turn around, she sticks her hand out. "I'm Ruby, the mother. And you must be Cole, the baby dad."

"I thought Ellery didn't want anyone to know," I say as we shake hands.

Juniper snorts. "You can't keep a secret from our mother. She was a Soviet spy in a previous life."

"Why Soviet? I couldn't have been a spy for my own country?" she grumbles as she sits down at the end of the row.

"Mrs. West is the high school principal. She does plenty of spying," Rowan explains.

Bang! Bang! Bang! Forest hits the table with a gavel before announcing, "Let's get this meeting started."

I push out a sigh of relief when I note his pet squirrel, Chip, is not in attendance. Chip's beady eyes freak me out. I swear he was plotting my death while he nibbled on my drawings the last time I saw him.

"I thought you were going to steal his gavel," Juniper whispers to Ashlyn.

"I did. He must have bought another one."

I ignore them since the meeting has finally commenced. My knees bounce up and down since my feet can't remain still now we've finally arrived at the moment when I learn if *Davis Williams* won the bid.

"Does anyone have any announcements before we begin?"

"Don't keep us in suspense, Forest!" a woman yells.

"Drink," Juniper orders.

"The word is not. Feather said don't, which is a contraction of do and not," Lilac explains.

Juniper grins. "Drink!"

"For goodness sake," Lilac mumbles as she sips on her beer.

"Yeah, Forest. Who won the bid?" another woman shouts.

A group of women begin chanting, "Who won the bid? Who won the bid? Who won the bid?"

"Those women are Feather, Petal, Cayenne, and Clove. Together with Sage who's getting a dressing down from Lyric." Rowan nods toward the hallway where Lyric is gesturing with his hands at Sage who's smiling back at him. "I refer to them as the gossip gals."

"They prefer the term busybody," Ashlyn tells him.

Doubts about what the hell I'm doing here creep in. Is making partner at the firm worth working in this crazy town for the next two years? What is my chance of convincing Ellery to relocate closer to Chicago with our child?

"She won't move," Juniper answers the question I didn't ask. "She built the *Inn on Main* from the ground up. It's her baby. You could offer her five million dollars for the place, and she'd turn you down."

"Remember the developer?" Aspen asks. "He offered her six and she told him where he could shove his six million."

Lilac purses her lips. "I don't remember any developer making an offer on the inn. Is this yet another secret you and Ellery are keeping from the rest of us?"

"Yeah, big sis, what other secrets are you keeping?" Ashlyn asks.

"My wife's a troublemaker." Rowan smiles at her as if he's proud of the trouble she gets herself into.

Bang! Bang! Bang!

Ashlyn grits her teeth. "I'm going to steal every gavel in town."

"Will everyone be quiet for five minutes, so I can announce who won the bid," Forest yells. Once everyone quiets down, he points his gavel at me. "Congrats!"

"The hunk won! The hunk won! The hunk won!" The gossip gals chant.

Lilac stands. "*Davis Williams* did not win the bid because Cole is the most handsome architect. They won because their design plan was the most ecologically sound."

"He's still a hunk!"

I stand, thinking I need to say something, but I don't get a chance to speak before I'm surrounded by the West family.

Mrs. West pulls me into her arms and rocks me back and forth. "Welcome to the family. This project will give you plenty of time to win Ellery over. She's stubborn. All my girls are," she says with pride. "But she needs love. And you'll do just fine." She winks as she releases me.

Rowan claps me on the back. "Welcome to the chaos."

Ashlyn throws herself at me, but Rowan grabs her by the collar and drags her away. "No hugging other men."

"He's practically family."

He shakes his head. "Not yet he isn't. And he's got his work cut out for him."

She melts into him. "Okay, Jeeves."

"I don't have a caveman who will keep me from hugging you." Juniper wraps her arms around me. "I get the attraction," she whispers as she pinches my ass.

I jump out of her arms. "Um..." I can feel my face heating up.

"Does everyone get to pinch his ass or is the privilege reserved for the West sisters?" Sage asks as she returns with Lyric.

Lyric sighs. "Unwanted pinching is assault. Don't make me arrest you."

Sage winks at me. "Who says it's unwanted?"

"Um..." What do you say when a woman old enough to be your grandmother wants to pinch you? I eye the exit. I need to get out of here before the entire town decides pinching my ass is the appropriate method to congratulate me.

Lilac pushes past Sage. "Congratulations." She holds out her hand. "I found your project inspired. I'd love to discuss it more at your convenience."

"Later," Aspen says. "It's time for drinks and a celebration at the bar."

Juniper hooks her arm through mine. "Come on. I'll keep the other women at bay."

"You have to go to the restroom sometime, Juniper," Sage calls after her.

"She's kidding, isn't she?"

Juniper grins up at me. "We can pretend she is if it makes you feel better."

Before I can come up with an answer to her crazy, Ashlyn sprints past with Rowan chasing her. "You can't catch me, I'm the gingerbread woman!"

Winter Falls is officially freaking me out.

Chapter Thirteen

"Are you going to stand on the porch all afternoon or are you coming inside?" Mom yells her question from inside her house.

I groan. It's Sunday, aka weekly dinner with the family time. I've tried to get out of the dinner before, but it wasn't worth the thirty-minute guilt trip Dad gave me when he showed up at the inn all disappointed I couldn't carve an hour's time out of my busy schedule for the family.

The way he says family you'd think we were in the Russian mob – Dad is a first generation American born to two Soviet defectors. But Dad assures me we're not Bratva, which disappoints Ashlyn to no end, because my baby sister is a nutter.

"I'm merely admiring the last of the sun on this winter's day."

I'm also freezing my ass off while I try to gather the courage to enter my childhood home where I need to confess to my parents I'm pregnant. Sigh. Best to get this over with.

I open the door and charge inside, but when my gaze lands on Cole, I freeze.

"What's he doing here?"

"He's family since he's your baby daddy. Because apparently, you didn't listen to my lecture about using prophylactics."

"Which one?" Ashlyn asks. "There were a lot."

I narrow my gaze on my sisters who are sitting on the sofa together as if they're watching a soap opera. I'm surprised they don't have popcorn. "Who told?"

Aspen giggles. "Are you serious? No one told. Mom can sniff out any and all secrets within a twenty-mile radius."

"Do you remember the time she showed up at the police station to bail us out and Lyric hadn't even rang her yet?" Ashlyn asks.

Juniper groans. "You and your 'great ideas'."

"It was a great idea. How was I to know Gratitude was still at the library? It was after midnight."

"Maybe because she never leaves the place. I think she sleeps in the basement."

"I don't know what the problem was. We weren't causing any trouble. I only wanted to read the book on how to perform a séance and communicate with the dead. She didn't need to tattle to the police on us."

"I don't understand why you dislike the librarian," Mom huffs. "Gratitude is a lovely person."

Ashlyn snorts. "Yeah. If you're the high school principal and paying her for all the gossip."

Mom sniffs. "I would never pay for gossip."

"You should probably escape while you have the chance," I tell Cole who's staring at my family with his mouth hanging open. At my words, his mouth snaps shut.

"I told you I'm not running. In case you haven't heard the news, my firm got the contract for the community center. You're going to be seeing a whole lot more of me."

Butterflies wake up in my stomach at his words. Knock it off, I tell them. It's winter. It's no time for butterflies. They ignore me. Naturally. I place a hand on my stomach to keep them quiet.

Cole's eyes brighten. "Can you feel the baby? Is she kicking?"

"*He*'s not kicking." I emphasize he to be contrary.

Lilac stands. "You're not feeling the baby yet." She frowns. "You're nineteen weeks pregnant. When is your mid-pregnancy ultrasound?"

"Whoa." I hold up my hands to ward her off. "Did you make a graph of my pregnancy?"

"Of course, not." Phew. "It's a chart." I retract my phew.

"Lilac," I growl.

"Can you email me a copy?" Mom asks.

"Me too!" Aspen agrees and pretty soon all of my sisters are chiming in to say they want a chart of the growth of my baby.

I cover my face with my hands. "Can't any of you pretend to be normal in front of a guest at least?" I mumble.

"He's no guest, sis." Lyric throws his arm around my shoulders. "According to your mom, baby daddies are family."

I shove him off of me. "Can everyone please stop using the phrase baby daddy?"

"Why?" Lilac glances back and forth between me and Cole. "Cole is the baby's daddy. Or is there another man we should know about?"

"I didn't know about this man," Aspen grumbles.

"And I didn't know you're a big fat idiot who actually thought Lyric would—"

She shoves her palm in my face. "We don't say her name," she hisses.

Dad lumbers into the room with Rowan on his heels. "What were you two up to?" I ask in a desperate attempt to change the topic of conversation from baby daddies and pregnancy charts.

Dad winks. "Manly business."

Mom snorts. "What kind of manly business can you conduct in the backyard? It's too cold to grill."

He kisses the tip of her nose. "None of your business, wife of mine."

I expect Mom to lay into him. She hates it when she doesn't know every single thing every person in town is up to. Thus, the whole knowing I'm pregnant thing. But she smirks at him. "We'll talk later."

"Ew. She's going to use sex to force him to tell her everything. Save me." Ashlyn buries her face in her hands.

Rowan picks her up from the sofa and pulls her into his arms. "I'll save you."

Ashlyn bites her lip and bats her eyelashes at him. "Will you wear a coat of mail and carry a sword?"

He leans close to whisper in her ear.

"What did you say? I couldn't hear you," Juniper says.

Ashlyn sticks her tongue out at Juniper. "Way to ruin a moment."

"The only reason I'm here is to make fun of my sisters and eat some homemade grub. You can at least make it worth my while to leave my animals."

"You do know the animals at the wildlife refuge aren't *your* animals, don't you?"

Juniper is in charge of caring for the animals at the wildlife refuge outside of town. The animals are mostly wild animals people thought would make great pets. But when they grow out of their cute and cuddly phase, they become dangerous animals and often end up at the refuge where Juniper coddles them.

Juniper frowns at Ashlyn. "They are my babies."

"Yeah. Because bobcats are such cuddly babies."

Cole tugs on my hand and electricity shoots up my arm toward my neck while my entire body warms at his touch. I yank out of his hold. I don't need to have warm and tingly feelings about a man who's going to leave me.

"Can we talk?"

"It depends. Do you want my entire family to hear our conversation?"

He glances over at my family who – sure enough – have halted whatever they were doing to observe us. He swallows. "We'll talk later."

I nod, despite having no intention of talking to him later. I may not have been very successful at avoiding him this past week, but I can do better. Besides, he now has the community center project to work on. Hopefully, he'll be too busy to play hide and seek with me.

Mom claps her hands. "Dinner is ready." She points to Cole. "You'll sit next to Ellery." She motions toward a chair.

I don't bother to grumble. There's no way I'm getting out of sitting next to him during dinner.

"How did you two meet?" Mom asks once everyone's seated and the food is being passed around.

Ashlyn rolls her eyes. "At the inn. Duh."

Rowan tweaks her nose. "I don't think your mom was asking you, dream girl."

She shrugs. "I'm just saying."

Cole presses his thigh against mine. I glance over to figure out what he's trying to communicate to me, but he's digging into his food. I scoot away and lose the connection with him. I don't miss the heat of his thigh pressing against mine. Not me.

Mom ignores her youngest child to ask, "Are you two a couple or merely co-parents?"

"We're not a couple," I'm quick to explain.

"Why not? Cole is your type."

Gee thanks, Mom. The last thing I need is the man thinking I'm into him. *You are into him,* my heart reminds me.

Aspen giggles. "If I had to draw a picture of the man Ellery would end up with, I'd draw a picture of Cole." I throw a roll at her and she catches it in the air. "Thanks."

"What about you?" Mom asks Cole.

He meets her gaze, and I notice a line of sweat break out on his forehead. Good. I'm not alone in feeling uncomfortable. "Me what?"

"Is Ellery your type? I mean, obviously, she's your type for a one-night stand since you got her pregnant. By the way, there's a bag of condoms for you at the door."

Cole's face heats and his eyes dart around the room. Don't look at me. I'm not bailing you out of this situation.

Rowan slaps him on the back. "Breathe, dude. Mrs. West gives everyone in the community condoms. I think she has stock in the condom company."

"She gave me a condom the first time I took Aspen out on a date." Lyric pauses. "We were fifteen."

"You can never be too early to learn about prophylactics," Mom sings.

Ashlyn groans. "When you don't know boys have penises yet, you're too young."

"No talking about other men's ..." Rowan cuts himself off.

"Pe-nis. Come on, Jeeves. You can say the word. Penis. Penis. Pe-nis."

Rowan slaps a hand over Ashlyn's mouth. "Knock it off, troublemaker."

I turn to Cole. "Are you sure you want to tangle yourself up in this family? This is a tame day for the West family."

He smiles and his dimple comes out to play. "I think I can handle it."

"It's your funeral."

I pretend to be indifferent when indifference is the furthest thing from my mind. Despite how good it feels to have Cole sitting next to me now, I don't want him to entangle himself in my family. It will only make things worse when he flees town never to return.

Chapter Fourteen

I grunt as I roll out of bed. I thought the heartburn was bad the day after Aspen dared me to drink chocolate peppermint martinis all night, but it has nothing on what I'm experiencing now. Who said pregnancy makes you glow? Whoever it was needs their butt kicked.

I trudge to the kitchen to heat up some milk. The smell of warm milk makes me want to gag, but I'm willing to try anything at the moment. I pause when I hear a door slam.

I check the clock. Two a.m. I know I closed and locked the rear 'employee' door to the inn when I quit work last night. Of course, guests are free to come and go as they please through the other entrances to the inn, but it's two a.m. on a Tuesday night. Nothing happens in Winter Falls at this time. Even the town bar, *Electric Vibes,* shuts at midnight during the week.

Milk forgotten, I shuffle to the window to peek outside. Despite the lack of street lights – street lights are akin to sacrilege in Winter Falls – I can see a bit since the moon is nearly full. And what I see has me rushing to the front door.

I shove my feet into a pair of boots and fling my door open before trudging down the stairs. I stomp toward my sisters who I am officially kicking out of the family this very minute. Aspen and Ashlyn are giggling to each other and don't hear me coming up behind them.

"What are you doing?"

Aspen screams while Ashlyn whirls around brandishing the shovel in her hands like it's a weapon.

"Geez, Ellery. I nearly took your head off. You could have warned us." Ashlyn drops the shovel and leans against the handle.

"Warn you? You're on my property in the middle of the night!" I hiss.

"Am I having a heart attack?" Aspen rubs her chest. "Oh no. I think I peed my pants."

"Keep it down. I have guests at the inn."

"I told you to wear the adult diapers," is Ashlyn's bizarre response.

"I'm not wearing adult diapers because it will be handy if we get arrested and they won't let us use the restroom. My husband is the Chief of Police."

"Fine. Ignore my advice. See if I care. And Lyric isn't your husband yet."

"Rowan isn't your husband yet either."

"I didn't say he was."

Is it wrong to wish you can hit your sisters with a shovel?

"Can you two have this argument elsewhere? I don't need the guests waking up and I need to get some sleep."

"Why are you awake?" Aspen asks. "It's the middle of the night. You should be in bed growing your baby."

Growing my baby? Since when is my baby a plant?

"Didn't you read Lilac's email? According to the chart, Ellery may be experiencing insomnia in her second and third trimester."

I groan. "What did Lilac the all-knowing send everyone?"

Ashlyn grins down at me. My 'little' sister is half a foot taller than me and she doesn't let me forget it either.

"It's basically a primer on everything to expect when you're expecting. Rowan found it very helpful."

Aspen's mouth drops open. "Are you trying?"

"Yep."

"I thought you wanted to wait until you're married."

Ashlyn shrugs. "I was teasing. We've been trying since the day he put his ring on my finger."

"But you're barely twenty-four. What's the rush?"

"I'm not making Rowan wait to have the family he wants. Not after what his bitch of an ex-wife did to him."

Aspen leans closer. "What did she do?" At least, she's whispering now.

"I can't tell you. You know how Rowan is about his privacy."

"Come on. It's me. Your big sister. He's practically family. I'm the aunt to his future children."

Ashlyn mimes zipping her lips shut. I'm amazed. Can my baby sister actually keep a secret? Miracles do happen.

"Can we continue the gossip session inside?"

Ashlyn throws the shovel over her shoulder. "Sorry, sis, but no. We've got a job to do."

"You are not digging in my front yard."

"We'll fill in any holes we make. Promise." Ashlyn bats her eyelashes. Does she actually think I'll fall for her innocent act? My baby sister hasn't been innocent since she learned to crawl and managed to make her way out of the living room into the pantry and lock herself in.

I was eight at the time, but I will never forget how Dad and Mom frantically searched the house for her. She was finally found when she started wailing because she was hungry. Although, how she could possibly be hungry when she devoured everything she could reach in the pantry is beyond me.

"But we know the Black Hat Bandit's missing loot is buried in your front yard."

I cross my arms over my chest. Not this again. "We know no such thing."

"But the newsletter article said we'd uncover the loot at the cornerstone of the mansion."

"Yeah, sis," Aspen pushes. "The loot has got to be here."

They're referring to a treasure hunt they've been on for the past months. In specific, they're searching for the fifty-thousand dollars the bank robber, the Black Hat Bandit, stole from the Hastings National Bank in Nebraska in 1955.

Aspen found a letter from the bandit's lover, Patricia Hall, when she was clearing out the storage room in her bookstore, *Fall Into A Good Book*, referring to the loot. Since then, the two of them have been on the hunt to find the money.

"The mansion was built in 1925. There's no way Robert Adams aka the bandit could have hid the money in the cornerstone. The building was already thirty years old when he came to town," I explain.

Based on their latest 'clue', they're convinced the loot is hidden in the cornerstone of *The Inn on Main*. They're out of their minds if they think I'm going to let them dig around my business on some wild goose chase.

"Maybe he hid the money in the ground in front of the cornerstone," Ashlyn suggests.

"You have to admit it's plausible," Aspen pushes.

I'm admitting no such thing. I cross my arms over my chest and Aspen gasps before rushing to me. I swat her away. "What is wrong with you?"

She indicates my stomach. "Your belly popped."

Ashlyn drops the shovel, and it clangs to the ground. She claps and bounces on her toes. "This is so exciting. I'm going to be an aunt."

Aspen elbows her. "I'm going to be the best aunt."

"Children," I hiss, "I have four sisters who are going to be aunts. Two of whom will be disowned if they don't quiet down and put away their shovels before any of my guests wake up."

Ashlyn picks up the shovel. "I'll put this away."

I follow her toward the garage under my apartment where I notice the door hanging open. "You couldn't have closed the door after you broke in?" I don't need any wild animals nesting in my garage.

"We weren't going to be long. Besides, no one heard us," Aspen claims.

"No one?"

"No one besides you, I mean."

I wait as Aspen and Ashlyn stow the shovel and trowel. Once they've locked up the garage, I wave and ascend the stairs toward my apartment. They follow me.

"What are you doing?" I ask them as I reach the door.

Aspen shrugs. "Isn't it obvious?"

"I thought it was," Ashlyn adds.

"It's the middle of the night. I need some sleep before I have to get up in three hours."

When they continue to stare at me, I give in and open my door. Ashlyn pushes past me. "I'll make the hot milk."

"Did Lilac include instructions for treating heartburn in her Ellery's pregnant treatise?" I grumble as I make myself comfortable on the sofa.

"You really should let us dig around," Ashlyn ignores my question to say. "As the owner of the land, the money would be yours. Minus a finder's fee, of course."

"I hope you're referring to my finder's fee," Aspen adds as she plops down next to me on the sofa.

Ashlyn's nose wrinkles. "Why is it yours? I'm the one who read Old Man Mercury's book about Winter Falls and figured out the brewery building is older than everyone thought. I'm also the one who figured out the clue in the letter from Robert to Patricia."

"You're marrying a millionaire. You don't need the money."

Ashlyn hands me a mug of milk. I sniff it and my stomach clenches.

"You and your aversion to warm milk. I didn't poison it."

"You didn't?" I ask to make certain.

"Not this time. And how was I supposed to know you'd steal Gratitude's drink?"

I shiver thinking about how much time I spent throwing up the contents of my stomach due to the ipecac syrup Ashlyn laced in the librarian's coffee.

"You need to get over your vendetta with the librarian," Aspen comments.

I force myself to down half of the milk in one go. "The same way you've gotten over yours with her?" To say the West sisters and the librarian have butted heads in the past is an understatement. A vast understatement.

"It's not a vendetta."

"Whatever," I mumble.

"Do we tell our children about all the crazy stuff we did as teenagers, or do we keep them in the dark?" Ashlyn wonders.

"I didn't do any crazy stuff," I claim.

"No one did as much crazy stuff as Ashlyn. Rowan will have his hands full when she starts pushing out babies."

I grunt because apparently, warm milk does make you drowsy. Who knew? Besides those websites recommending warm milk I mean.

Aspen throws a blanket over me. "Get some sleep, Ellery. We'll talk later."

I hear them let themselves out of my apartment, but I don't bother to open my eyes as sleep pulls me under.

Chapter Fifteen

Cole

I patiently wait behind the line of people checking in at the inn to speak to Ellery. She's been avoiding me since Sunday dinner with her family and I'm done with it. Whether she likes it or not, I'm the father of her child. We will always be in each other's lives.

When it's my turn, Ellery glances up with a smile on her face. The smile freezes when she notices it's me. "How may I help you, Mr. Hawkins?"

Mr. Hawkins? Does she think using my last name is somehow going to discourage me? She obviously doesn't know me very well – which is the entire problem.

I smile, making sure my dimple pops out. I'm not an idiot. I know she finds my dimple attractive. I'm not above using her attraction to me to get what I want.

"First off, you can call me Cole."

She frowns. "Cole. How may I help you?"

"You can accompany me to the Yule celebrations this weekend."

There are no Christmas celebrations in Winter Falls. No, they celebrate Yule instead. I'd claim their celebrations are for the benefit of tourists but having met some of the hippies who live here, I find it difficult to believe they'd do anything on behalf of tourists.

"I'm working all weekend."

I feel a muscle tick in my jaw. She works entirely too hard. Especially since she's pregnant. I can't mention her pregnancy, though. She doesn't want anyone to know about it. But I noticed she started wearing her blouses untucked from her pants last week. It won't be long before she'll have to tell people or they'll guess.

"How about this evening? After all the guests are checked in?"

She sighs. "I need to be here in case anyone needs anything."

"What about Moon?" I motion to the woman strolling into the hallway from the kitchen.

Moon grimaces. "Sorry, Cole. I work at the brewery tonight. Considering the celebrations, I can't cancel last minute."

Ellery beams up at me. She opens her mouth to speak – she's not above bragging – but Moon gets there before she does.

"Although, Soleil can come in. She's not working the festival tonight." She winks at me. "I'll message her." She bounces off.

"I guess we're going to the celebrations tonight," I tell Ellery and stroll off before she can come up with another excuse.

Ellery manages to get the last word in, nonetheless. She messages me at dinnertime to let me know she can't meet up until nine due to an 'emergency'. Apparently, being a scaredy cat is now an emergency. I don't know what her problem is with me, but I'm determined to figure it out.

I arrive at her apartment half an hour early. When I knock on the door and there's no answer, I peek in the window to discover her asleep on the sofa. Shit. I can hardly wake her. We need to talk, but she needs her sleep more. I begin creeping backwards toward the stairs.

Her phone alarm beeps, her eyes fly open, and she looks around in confusion. She appears adorable all tired and confused. I want to pick her up and carry her to bed. Not for sex – although sex is always welcome – but to cuddle next to her as she catches up on some much-needed sleep.

She picks up her phone and swears. "I'm late. Cole is going to kill me."

Looks like I'll be taking her out tonight after all. I brush the snow off the chair on her porch and settle in to wait for her to get ready. At ten minutes to nine, the door flies open and Ellery rushes out. She skids to a stop when she notices me.

"I thought we were meeting at the front desk."

I stand and hold out my elbow. "Just being a gentleman." And making sure she doesn't sneak out on me.

She stares at my elbow for several seconds before sighing and lacing her arm through mine. "Let's get this over with."

I chuckle. "Calm down. I'm not sure I can handle this level of excitement."

She rolls her eyes at me, but there's a smile on her face and I realize I want all of her smiles directed at me.

"Where to?" I ask once we've descended the stairs.

"The parade begins at ten. We can watch it from in front of Aspen's bookstore. It's on the other side of Main Street. We'll probably need an hour to make our way there."

An hour to make it the half mile to the other side of town? She must be joking. When we reach the street side of the inn, I understand what she means. Main Street is packed with people strolling up and down through town. The atmosphere resembles a carnival with food booths and games scattered throughout the street.

"Do you want to play a game?" She motions toward the whack-a-mole where her sister Ashlyn is standing with Rowan.

I pay for two tickets and pick up my mallet. Ellery takes a position next to me while Ashlyn and Rowan are across from us.

"Ready. Set. Go."

The first mole pops up except it's not a mole. It's gone before I can figure it what it is.

"What the hell was that thing?"

"Duh. It's an oil rig." Ellery's mallet doesn't pause as she explains to me. "Moles are animals. We don't harm animals in Winter Falls. But oil rigs? Those we can harm."

The machine beeps to announce time's up and Ashlyn's station lights up to indicate she's the winner. She throws her hands in the air in victory. Her hands which both contain mallets. I don't need to ask how Ashlyn won.

"You can't bring an extra whack thingamabob!" Ellery yells at her before stomping toward her sister where she yanks the extra mallet out of her hands before whacking her sister with it.

"Hey! Stop it." Ashlyn reaches up to pull Ellery's hair, and I force my way in between the two of them.

"Are you crazy?" I hiss at her. "Your sister is pregnant. You can't fight her."

"Wait until I'm pregnant," Ashlyn announces, "then, you won't be able to touch me."

"But you're not pregnant yet," Rowan says in a loud voice and several heads turn in our direction.

"You didn't have to tell the entire world we're trying to have a baby!" Ashlyn screeches at him ensuring everyone who didn't hear Rowan the first time now knows.

Rowan shrugs. "You already told your sisters."

While the two argue, I tag Ellery's hand and lead her away. "Are you okay? She didn't hurt you, did she?"

"Ashlyn's harmless unless you're the librarian."

I don't want to know. "Do you want to get a bite to eat, or do you want to play another game?"

"I want to play the goldfish toss."

I raise an eyebrow. "It's not okay to whack a pretend mole, but it is okay to throw ping pong balls at real, live fish?"

She rolls her eyes. "Who said anything about fish?"

A goldfish toss without fish? This I gotta see. "Lead the way."

She grasps my hand and my heart swells at the unconscious act. As much as she wants to deny it, Ellery likes me. She guides me toward another carnival booth. She fishes in her pocket for money, but I'm not letting her pay. Whether she wants it to be or not, this is a date. I pay for six chances and hand her half of the ping pong balls.

"Or would you rather I take all the chances?"

"How about a little wager?"

"Oooo, what are we wagering? A little sexy time between the sheets? I have some candles you should try," Petal interrupts to say.

"Cole and I aren't involved."

My heart clenches at her words. I know we're not in a relationship but hearing her say the truth hurts. I wanted to explore the future with Ellery before I knew she was pregnant. Now she's carrying our baby, I'm determined more than ever to convince her to take a chance on me.

"And I think I've bought enough candles from you." One candle was enough considering it was a sex candle and I had no idea.

Petal cackles and her husband draws her away. "Come on, darling. Let's let the young people have their fun."

"But you know I enjoy watching," she pouts.

"What do you want to wager?" I ask Ellery once we're alone again.

She taps her chin as she studies me. "How about you help clean the toilets tomorrow if you lose?"

"And if I win?"

She shrugs. "Winner's choice."

"Let's do this." I'm not telling her what I want before we begin because she's liable to run away if I tell her I want to talk to her. Really talk to her about the future of our baby. Of us.

I throw my first ball expecting it to sink into the water of the fish bowl except it bounces out when it hits the contents of the bowl. I scowl. "What's in the bowls? It's obviously not water."

She smirks. "Candy canes. Feather makes them in the winter to supplement her income from the ice cream shop."

She throws a ball, and it lands perfectly in one of the bowls. Shit. 1-0 for Ellery. I don't give up easily, though.

I toss again, this time lobbing the ball softly to ensure it doesn't bounce out of the bowl.

"1-1," I say to her when my ball stays in the bowl.

Her nose scrunches up as she concentrates on throwing another ball. This one hits the side of a bowl and falls to the floor.

The score is now tied and we each have one ball left. I toss my ball and hold my breath as it lands in the bowl. It bounces before dropping back.

"2-1. Your turn."

"Prepare to clean those toilets," she says as she throws her ball. It lands in a bowl on the opposite side of us.

"Yes!" She punches her fist into the air, but her arm freezes when the ball bounces up and out of the bowl.

"You were saying."

"Best of six."

"Nope. You can't change the wager after we've begun." And I'm not losing the chance to have a serious discussion with her.

"You're carrying the bowls," she grumps as the manager hands me three fish bowls filled with miniature candy canes.

I follow her as she stomps to Aspen's bookstore where the rest of the West family is gathered. We settle into our seats, and I lean over to whisper to her. "Are you going to be grumpy for the rest of the night?"

I watch as goosebumps break out on her skin in response to my breath wafting over her skin. Ellery is as affected by me as I am by her. Maybe this conversation we need to have won't be so bad after all.

Chapter Sixteen

My hands shake as I try to slot the key into the lock at my apartment. Unlike other Winter Falls residents, I am a big believer in always locking my door. I have four sisters who don't understand what personal boundaries are. I'd be a fool to keep my door unlocked, although a locked door doesn't do much to keep them out some days.

Cole places his hand on my lower back to steady me. His touch is anything but steadying. Instead of calming me, it's as if electricity rushes out of his fingertips to my back and through my body. I close my eyes and inhale a steadying breath before I decide to spin around and jump the man.

My keys fall to the porch, and he bends to pick them up before reaching over me to unlock the door. Since he's more than half a foot taller than me, it's not a difficult feat. Great Scott! The guy's a giant compared to me. What does this mean for the baby growing inside me? I latch onto the fear with both hands. Anything to forget the mini-shocks still traveling through my body from his touch.

"What's wrong?"

"I didn't say anything was wrong."

He repeats his question instead of calling me the liar I obviously am. "What's wrong?"

I throw my arms in the air. "You're a giant! What if our child is your size? My body will never recover."

The idea of forcing a watermelon out of my body is already less than appealing. But what if the watermelon is some humongous mutant watermelon?

He laughs as he opens the door and guides me inside. "I'm not a giant, although you may be a midget."

I throw daggers at him with my eyes. "I'm five-foot-two. I am not a midget and referring to a person as a midget is offensive. Thank you for escorting me home."

"Are you kicking me out?"

"What was your first clue?"

"Don't you want to know what I want since I won our little bet?"

He knows I do. He's been teasing me all night about it.

I shrug. "You can tell me tomorrow."

He smirks and steps closer. My nipples tighten and tingles travel down my body until they reach my core. Maybe he wants sex. I am on board with this plan. I can have this dress off and his pants around his ankles in seconds.

I fist my hands. *Stop it, Ellery.* I am not having sex with my baby daddy and complicating an already complicated relationship. Great. Now, I'm calling Cole my baby daddy.

He lowers his voice an octave before asking, "You sure you don't want to know?"

Damn him. He knows his husky voice lights me on fire. "Enough with the teasing," I manage to croak out. "What do you want for winning?"

He grasps my hand and leads me to the sofa. "Maybe you should sit down for this."

My eyes widen. I need to sit down? He doesn't mean— He couldn't possibly think—

"Calm down, Ellie. I'm not going to force you to have sex with me."

He's not? Bummer. No. Wait. I don't want sex with the man. And I'm not a big fat liar. Good thing I'm wearing a dress because my pants would totally be on fire now.

"What do you want?" I ask as I sit down.

He perches on the edge of my coffee table in front of me. "I want to talk."

I groan. "What about what I want?"

He squeezes my hands. "You know we need to talk about the baby."

"I know." My lips purse. "It doesn't mean I want to."

"Whether you like it or not, I am this child's father. Nothing will ever change that. You living in Winter Falls. You getting married." He frowns. "Whatever happens, this child is mine."

"Ours," I interrupt to say because he is completely freaking me out.

He dips his chin. "Ours." He clears his throat. "I want to be involved in everything from now on."

"Everything?"

He nods. "Ultrasounds. Doctor's visits. Whatever you need to do, I want to be there."

"We use midwives here in Winter Falls," I say to be contrary.

"Okay. Midwife appointments."

"Are you going to be my Lamaze partner, too?" I'd change my mind and endure Lamaze classes with Cayenne the contortionist just to witness his reaction.

"Whatever you need. I'm here."

Here? Wrong thing to say. It reminds me of why I can't trust him.

"Exactly! You aren't here. You're not a local."

"I know you don't like outsiders."

"It's not that I don't like outsiders." I don't trust them. It's an entirely different thing.

"Winter Falls is going to be my base of operations for the next two years."

"And then what?" I can't help myself from pushing. "Then, you're gone and we never hear from you again."

A muscle in his jaw twitches and a vein in his forehead pulses. "I would never abandon my child. Never."

He sounds sincere, but, "How do I know you won't?"

He leaps to his feet and starts pacing my living room. He circles the room for a few minutes while mumbling to himself. Finally, he stops in front of me.

"I would never abandon my child because I know how it feels to be abandoned."

What is he talking about? "Say what?"

"It's such a cliché it's almost funny. My dad went to the grocery store to pick up some milk for me and he never came back."

"Never? He left your mom?"

"My mom. Me. He left our lives and never looked back again."

"What an asshole!" I slap a hand over my mouth. "Sorry. I shouldn't have said your dad is an asshole."

He waves my apology away. "It's not a word I haven't used myself in reference to him a million times before."

"Do you ever hear from him? Does he write? Did he visit for the holidays?" Shit. All these years I've yelled at the residents of Winter Falls for being nosey and I'm doing the exact same thing. "Never mind. You don't need to tell me. It's your business."

"Nuh-uh. No giving me the brush off. It's our business. Because my father abandoning his family and never speaking to me again is the reason why you can trust me to never abandon our child. I know how it feels to be the person left behind. I would never treat a person that way, let alone my child."

Wow. What can I say? How can I begin to understand when I grew up in a loving family? An irritating family but loving, nonetheless.

"Do you want a drink?" I don't wait for his answer before walking to the sink to pour a glass of water.

"I'm sorry," he apologizes when I hand him the glass of water.

"Sorry? For what?"

"Sorry, our child won't have four grandparents."

I snort. "Have you met my parents? My mom won't have any trouble filling in any gaps left by your father. My dad's parents are still alive as well. They're Russian immigrants and will smother their first great-grandchild in love and worry."

"I can't wait to meet them."

Oh boy. I forgot about him meeting them. Babushka loves to 'test' new members of the family. Mom and her get along like ants on fire now, but Mom's told us the story of how they met. Gulp.

"What about the rest of your family?" I ask before my thoughts can spiral any further.

He finishes his water and sets the glass on the counter before answering. "There isn't much. I'm a single child. My mother never remarried. Her parents died when she was young. I have an uncle, my sister's older brother, but we're not in touch. He blames my mom for her husband leaving her, since he warned her about him."

"What a jerk. You don't abandon family because they don't do what you want. I wouldn't have any sisters left if I did."

He nods. "I know, which is why I will never abandon our child."

"I believe you." And I do believe him. Our child will be the top priority in Cole's life. I can see it plainly now.

But here comes the rub – the real reason I've been claiming I don't know what I'll do about the baby when there's no chance in hell I'd let anyone else in the world raise my child – I can't be certain *I* will be Cole's priority, too. And having Cole in my life only for him to return to Chicago where he does who knows what with another woman will hurt.

It shouldn't hurt. I barely know the guy after all. But I prefer not to lie to myself – too much. My heart is entangled and it's going to sting like a bitch when Cole shows up for our child with another woman on his arm.

I'm not about to tell Cole any of these thoughts, though. It won't change anything. He'll still abandon Winter Falls the second the community center is built. But I can't refuse to allow him to be a part of this child's life. Especially not after everything he's told me. I need to woman up.

He cradles my face. "Good. Does this mean you'll stop avoiding me now?"

I nod and his face descends. I hold my breath, but his lips don't meet mine. He kisses my forehead and I nearly swoon at the sweet gesture.

"And we'll get to know each other? Become friends?"

"Okay," I rasp.

"Good. Let me know when your next baby appointment is," he says before dropping his hands and strolling out the door.

Welp. Apparently, I've decided to go for a ride on the highway commonly referred to as heartbreak road.

Chapter Seventeen

I'm feeling thankful for the snowy weather as I throw on a bulky sweater before making my way to the monthly business meeting. Since my belly popped, I know I need to tell the people of Winter Falls about my pregnancy, but I'm not ready. Not ready for all the questions, offers of advice, and million tips about raising a baby.

But mostly, I'm not ready for questions about me and Cole. Are we together? Will he co-parent? Will he relocate to Winter Falls? The only thing I know is he won't abandon this baby. The rest? Damned if I know. I know what I want, but Cole staying in Winter Falls is a fool's dream.

As soon as I enter the meeting room in city hall, Ashlyn waves me over to where my sisters are sitting in the front row as usual. She presses a bottle of beer in my hands.

"Today's word is never."

"I can't drink," I hiss at her.

"It's non-alcoholic."

I sigh. "Must you play these childish games at every meeting?"

Ashlyn and Juniper invented a game where they drink every time anyone in the meeting says the word of the day. They claim the meetings needed livening up. As if anything in Winter Falls is ever boring.

"Don't tell me you're becoming a stick in the mud." Ashlyn scrunches her nose. "Do we need to rename you Uptight Number Three?"

Aspen's Uptight Number One, and Lilac's Uptight Number Two. It's obvious why Lilac's been dubbed uptight – my middle sister wrote the book on being rigidly conventional – but I don't know why Aspen has.

Juniper offers me some popcorn. "Want some?"

My stomach rumbles at the smell of butter and salt, and I snatch the bucket from her. "Thanks."

"If we can get this meeting started now," Forest booms from the front of the room.

"Where's his gavel?" I ask Ashlyn.

She widens her eyes and rears back. "Why are you asking me?"

I snort. "Don't come crying to me for bail money."

"Don't worry. I have connections with the police department." She winks.

Aspen reaches across me to slap Ashlyn. "Stop abusing my husband."

"Still not your husband," she sings.

Mom and Dad slip into the row behind us. Mom's hair is in disarray and her lipstick is smeared. No need to ask why they're late. Rowan and Cole sit next to them, and I wave at Cole because I promised to grow up and stop hiding from him. He winks and my body asks if we can hide somewhere *with* him.

"As this is our last meeting of the year, it's time to pick the mayor for next year," Forest announces, and I return my attention to the meeting before deciding my body has the right idea.

"Pick?" Cole asks.

"We don't elect a mayor. The mayor is drawn from the names of business owners out of a hat," Rowan explains.

Aspen crosses all of her fingers and begins to chant as she rocks in her seat with her eyes closed. "Don't be me. Don't be me. Don't be me."

Lilac rolls her eyes before standing and joining Forest at the front of the room.

"Winter Falls should hire Lilac to be the mayor. She does all the work anyway." Lilac handles the finances of Winter Falls and is the person everyone goes to when there's a question about the town charter.

"Shush your mouth," Ashlyn hisses and slaps my shoulder. "Lilac's head is big enough already."

"My head is perfectly proportional to my body," Lilac answers from the front of the room because Ashlyn can't whisper to save her life.

"Can I have your attention, please?" Lilac scans the room, and everyone immediately quiets down. No one wants to get on the wrong side of the woman who controls the town's purse strings.

"We will now pick next year's mayor. The same rules apply as always. If your name is picked, you cannot turn the position down unless you were the mayor in the previous year. It is, however, allowed to procure a substitute. The substitute will not be compensated in any way." She narrows her eyes on Saffron.

"Why are you singling me out? I maintain gifting a person a copy of the *Kama Sutra* is not compensation." Except Saffron owned the bookstore before Aspen bought it from her a few months ago and giving someone a product from your store for free is pretty much the definition of bribery.

"And I paid for the dang copy in the end anyway," Lennon, the owner of the bar *Electric Vibes,* yells from the back.

"What are they talking about?" Aspen asks.

I wave away her question. "It was when you were off in Dallas."

"Would anyone like to double check all of the business owners' names are in the hat?" Lilac asks.

Laughter erupts in the room. Everyone knows better than to double check Lilac's work. Someone does not appreciate her work being questioned.

She holds the hat out to Forest. "If you would do the honors."

He rummages around in the hat for a while.

"Come on, Forest. Just pick one," is shouted from the back.

"Yeah. At this rate, I'll be in a nursing home before the next mayor is announced," someone else adds.

"Patience is a virtue," Lilac sings.

I giggle. "It's hard to believe Lilac grew up in the same town as us sometimes."

Forest picks a name and hands it to Lilac.

"Finally!" Ashlyn yells. "I thought he'd never pick a name."

Juniper raises her beer. "Drink!" When I don't raise my bottle, she glares at me. Fine. Whatever. I take a sip. Yuck. Non-alcoholic beer is gross.

"The new major for the upcoming year is ..." Lilac glances briefly at me before announcing, "Ellery West."

I spring to my feet. "I'm..." Shit. I can't turn down the position unless I tell the entire town I'm pregnant.

Ashlyn jumps to her feet next to me. "I volunteer as tribute! I volunteer as tribute!" She winks at Mom. "Reading those books came in handy after all."

"What's this all about?" Feather asks.

"Is Ashlyn volunteering because Ellery's pregnant?" Sage asks.

I gasp. "You know I'm pregnant?"

"Darling girl, we're not idiots. Of course, we know," Petal says while the rest of her gossip girl gang – Feather, Sage, Cayenne, and Clove – nod.

I throw my arms in the air. "You didn't have to tell the entire town!"

Forest raises his hand. "I knew."

"Me too," Basil yells from the back.

I glare at Dad. "You told."

"I'm going to be a grandpa."

Yep. He told.

"Why do you think we gave the contract for the community center to Cole's firm?" Clove asks.

Lilac slams her fist down on the table. "Someone doesn't need a gavel," Ashlyn mutters.

"I am going to explain this one last time. *Davis Williams* did not win the contract for the recreational center project because Cole is the father of Ellery's baby."

I bury my face in my hands and groan.

Juniper pats my back. "Don't be upset. I think everyone figured out Cole's the baby daddy before Ellery announced it to the town."

"Can we stop saying baby daddy now? I'm not a sixteen-year-old who accidentally got pregnant."

"But it was an accident you got pregnant, wasn't it?" Mom asks. "I know I taught you better about how to properly use prophylactics."

My face warms at the memory of her showing me and my sisters how to roll a condom on a banana. "Thanks, Mom. I don't think everyone in Winter Falls knew my being pregnant was an accident yet."

Cayenne laughs. "Naturally, we knew it was an accident. Ellery Promise West plans everything in her life. There's no way you'd be pregnant on purpose unless you were married."

Great. She makes me sound like the most boring person in the world. I glance over my shoulder to gauge Cole's response. He's sitting on the edge of his seat and eyeing the door. Uh oh.

"Maybe we should stop talking about my condition and continue the meeting now?"

Lilac clears her throat. "I agree." I blow out a breath in relief upon her words. "We'll discuss Ellery's condition at the bar after the meeting." There goes any relief I was feeling.

"Someone can crown me mayor now." Ashlyn joins Lilac at the front of the room. "I am ready to serve my people." She bows.

"This is going to be a blast," Juniper says before tossing a wad of popcorn in her mouth.

"Blast? I think you mean disaster."

She shrugs. "Blast? Disaster? It's all the same when Ashlyn's involved. Do you think Lyric would arrest the mayor?"

"Where is my husband?" Aspen asks as she searches the room.

"Did you elope without telling anyone?"

Aspen's shoulders slump. "No. Lyric won't elope."

"Then, you're not married." I bump her shoulder. "And you don't want to elope. You want to beat Ashlyn to the alter is all."

She frowns. "It's not fair my little sister got engaged a few weeks after me. It's bad enough you're having a baby before me."

I rub my belly. "Not on purpose."

Cole squeezes my shoulder. "Accident or not. This baby will never be treated as if she's a mistake."

"I think you mean *he*."

Bang! Bang! Bang! Ashlyn pounds a gavel on the table. I knew she stole Forest's gavel.

"I now declare myself mayor of Winter Falls. This meeting is adjourned. Let's party!"

Juniper rubs her hands together. "And so, the fun begins."

Ashlyn sprints past us, but I stop her. "Hey, baby sister."

She whirls around. "I think you mean, Madam Mayor."

I roll my eyes. "Thanks for volunteering."

"Are you kidding? I've been waiting my entire life to use the whole 'I volunteer as tribute'-thing."

"In that case, I'm glad I could assist you."

She waves before running off and jumping on Rowan's back. "To the bar, Jeeves!"

"Are we sure Ashlyn wasn't adopted?" I ask as I watch her pretend to whip Rowan.

Aspen threads her arm through mine. "Let's go. It's time for the inquisition."

"Can we skip it? Maybe you can create a diversion."

She ignores me. I knew she would. I wasn't exactly helpful in distracting the town when they decided to play matchmaker with Lyric and Aspen. She should thank me. She's bursting with happiness at being engaged to the man she's been in love with since second grade.

I scan the area for anyone who can be of assistance and notice Cole slip out the side door. Lucky bastard.

Chapter Eighteen

I open the door to my apartment several hours later to discover my sisters gathered in my living room.

"Now what?" If my question sounds snarky, it's because it is.

"You didn't honestly think you could sneak out of the bar without repercussion, did you?" Juniper asks.

"Yeah! We were celebrating my appointment as mayor. You can't miss it," Ashlyn adds.

I collapse on the sofa and lay my head back against the cushions. "I didn't escape to go have fun or – you know – catch up on my sleep because I'm pregnant or to have some time to deal with how everyone in town knows I'm pregnant despite my not telling them."

Aspen giggles. "You didn't seriously think you were keeping your pregnancy a secret, did you?"

"You didn't know until I was four months."

Lilac raises her hand. "I knew."

Ashlyn slaps her shoulder. "And yet you didn't tell us."

"You didn't ask." Lilac does not ascribe to the 'an omission is a lie'-team

"Anyway," I say loudly to stop all the talk of who knew what when, "I had to deal with a plumbing emergency."

Aspen shivers. "Don't tell me someone tried to flush their underwear again."

"Nope. A watch."

"How do you flush a watch?" Lilac's not being nosey. She's genuinely curious.

I shrug. "No idea. When I fished the watch out of the toilet, the guest was all 'So that's where my watch went.' Idiot."

"Some people are negligent when it comes to handling their things with care. And it doesn't matter how much the thing costs." Juniper shakes her head.

"Are you talking about—"

"No!" Juniper barks to cut off Ashlyn's question. Someone has a secret. I wonder what it is.

"What—"

"No!" I guess Juniper isn't open to talking.

I check the clock. It's after eleven. "I'm exhausted. My bed is screaming my name. Can whatever this is wait until morning?"

"We'll be quick," Aspen says.

I motion for her to proceed.

"You're being a bitch and as your sisters, it's our duty in life to inform you of when you're being a bitch. You need to give Cole a chance."

I rear back at Aspen's declaration. I'm being a bitch. What?

"We know you have this hang-up about Bob, who sounds like a tool by the way."

At Lilac's statement, I narrow my eyes on her. "How do you know?"

"He wasn't difficult to locate."

"Please tell me you're not harassing him online."

"Define harassing."

Yep. She's harassing Bob online. And you know what? I don't have the energy to care.

"Ooooh." Ashlyn rubs her hands together. "Do tell. Are you having dildos delivered to him?"

"Dildos? But he's a heterosexual man and ...." Lilac cuts herself off when it dawns on her how embarrassing it would be for Bob to receive a dildo in the mail. "I'll add it to my list. It's better than sending him Hawaiian pizzas."

"He hates pineapple."

Lilac's smile is downright evil. "Exactly."

"I signed him up for Grindr."

I gawk at Aspen. "You're joking!"

She shrugs. "It's nothing more than he deserves."

"Has he had any matches?" Ashlyn asks.

"What do you do? Pose as him and then set him up on real life dates?" Juniper asks.

"What an excellent idea," Aspen mumbles as she makes a note in her phone.

"Are you guys nuts? Bob is not worth going to jail for."

"You need to get over your aversion to jail. It's not so bad."

I stare at my baby sister. "Exactly how many times have you gone to jail?"

"Let me check." Lilac pulls out her phone. "I have a list."

Ashlyn smacks the phone out of Lilac's hand. "You have a list? Have you been spying on me?"

"It's not spying when the information is freely available to the public."

Aspen claps. "We've handled the Bob situation. Now, it's your turn to give Cole a chance."

I debate continuing to mislead them for a while but then a yawn hits me. I really am tired.

"Cole and I already talked. We're going to get to know each other and work on becoming friends for the baby's sake." And hopefully, I won't get my heart broken beyond repair when he departs Winter Falls for good.

"You have got to—" Ashlyn freezes. "Wait. Did you say you're going to be friends with your baby daddy?"

"She did." Aspen's forehead scrunches as she studies me. "She didn't say why she changed her mind, though."

I shrug. "I thought about it and realized I don't want to be at odds with the father of my child."

"You're a big, fat liar."

I gasp at Aspen's declaration. "How dare you?"

She wags a finger at me. "I have no doubt you spent some time thinking about it."

Juniper snorts. "Someone's an overthinker." I glare at her. "What? This can't be news to you."

"Ahem. May I continue?" I motion for Aspen to get on with whatever she has to say. "There's more to the story. You didn't suddenly wake up one day and decide to stop avoiding Cole."

"I never hid from him."

Ashlyn laughs. "I guess Moon was hallucinating when she found you hiding under your desk."

Dang. Moon saw? And she told Ashlyn?

"I don't know if having Moon work at the inn is such a good idea."

"Ladies!" Lilac shouts. "Can we return to the topic at hand?"

"And the topic is…" I'm not being evasive, I've seriously lost the plot.

"Why did you change your mind about Cole?"

I sigh. If I want to sleep tonight, I'm going to have to give them something. "Cole told me about his past and it made me realize I needed to give him a chance to be a father to this baby."

Ashlyn leans close. "Ooooo... His past. Tell us more."

"It's Cole's story to tell. Ask him if you want to know."

"But we tell you everything," she pouts.

I widen my eyes. "Really? You told me why you feel obligated to give Rowan a baby as quick as can be?"

"Rowan values his privacy."

"And Cole doesn't? He may not be a former professional football player, but he's still allowed to keep his life private."

"It's interesting how Cole thinks he's going to keep his background private from his family." Aspen smirks. "It's going to be fun to watch him realize how little privacy this family allows."

"I could do some research," Lilac offers.

"No! You will not go searching around the dark web to uncover Cole's every secret."

"Don't be silly. I wouldn't need the dark web for this search."

"Holy cow," Ashlyn whispers. "When did Uptight Number Two become cool? The dark web? I'm in the throes of a major girl crush right now."

Lilac frowns at Ashlyn. "No. Whatever you're thinking, forget it. I am not using my skills to help you hack into your college alma mater and change all your grades in your transcripts."

"I have other ideas."

Juniper snorts. "She's not going to steal rocket fuel for you either."

"Definitely not."

"My sisters are boring," Ashlyn huffs.

I stand. "This boring sister needs to get some rest now." I motion toward the door.

"At least we can talk about the baby to everyone now. It was killing me keeping it to myself," Ashlyn mumbles as she starts for the door.

"You didn't keep it to yourself. You told Rowan."

She whirls around. "No, big sister, I did not. Rowan knew before me because Lyric told him."

Aspen holds up her hands. "Don't get mad at me. I accept no responsibility or liability for the actions of my husband."

"Fiancé!" Juniper corrects.

"Besides," Lilac says, "when you're Lyric's wife, you will be financially responsible for any debts he incurs during your marriage unless you have a prenuptial agreement. Are you planning to have a prenup? It's probably a good idea since you own a business."

"I'm not having a prenup," Ashlyn says.

Juniper snorts. "Rowan's an idiot. He should definitely keep your grubby hands away from his millions."

"Hey! I don't have grubby hands." Ashlyn lifts her hands to show off their cleanliness.

I herd the lot of them out of my door. I can still hear them arguing after I shut and lock the door.

"As if a locked door can keep us out!" Aspen shouts from the other side of the door.

Shit. She's right. I put the chain on and engage the security system. I rest my forehead against the door for a second before forcing my legs to get in gear. The last thing I need is to wake up with a crick in my neck from falling asleep on the couch. Again. Bed it is.

My sisters may have left tonight without too much of a fight, but they're not going to leave me in peace about Cole. They're going to try their hands at matchmaking the two of us. And they have the whole town to support them. I probably should warn Cole, but what if he tells me not to worry? That he doesn't want me romantically anyway? Better to avoid the topic all around.

Chapter Nineteen

Cole

I inhale deeply through my nose before I lose my shit. Ellery is five months pregnant with a growing baby bump. Yet she somehow thinks she's going to shovel the snow from the porch and steps at the inn. I predict a hell of a lot of frustration in my life for the next four months plus eighteen years.

"Please let me shovel the snow." I'm literally begging to do work for her.

Ellery glares at me for a few seconds before throwing the shovel at me. "If you're this intent on shoveling snow, have at it."

"Thank you."

It galls me to thank the woman who's carrying my baby for allowing me to shovel her steps and sidewalk, but I keep a pleasant demeanor on my face. The woman is the very definition of stubborn. I'm not getting anywhere with her by pushing and prodding her.

When Ellery goes back inside, I begin shoveling snow from the porch as Ashlyn wraps holly around the banister.

"Isn't it late to put up Christmas decorations?"

"We don't put up Christmas decorations in Winter Falls until after Yule."

"Is Yule always around the Winter Solstice?" I ask since I didn't know Yule existed except as a lyric in *Deck the Halls* until a few days ago. I always assumed it was one of those archaic terms no longer applicable to modern society. Like good King Wenceslas and the Feast of Stephen.

"Yep."

She climbs onto the banister, and I drop my shovel to rush to her. I grab her legs before lifting her and placing her on solid ground again.

"Are you trying to kill yourself?"

"Why does everyone keep asking me that?"

"Maybe because your actions are reckless," I suggest.

She rolls her eyes at me. "You break one ankle—"

"Did you forget about the time you broke your arm climbing in a tree?" Ellery asks as she steps onto the porch carrying a tray.

Ashlyn giggles. "How could I forget? Lyric burst out of the treehouse with his pants around his ankles. He was terrified I'd hurt myself." She snorts. "But Aspen was pissed I'd interrupted them."

"You're a terror," I tell her.

She bows. "Thank you."

Ellery hands me a mug of hot chocolate. "My dad says the same thing about baby cakes." My heart clutches at the idea of being compared to her father. A man she loves with all her heart and considers a wonderful parent.

"Where's my drink?" Ashlyn asks Ellery while I try not to hyperventilate.

Ellery hands her a mug, but when Ashlyn sips on her drink she makes a face. "What the hell? This is hot chocolate."

"What did you expect? Whiskey?"

"Is a peppermint patty too much to ask for?"

Ellery cocks her brow. "I thought you were trying to get pregnant."

Ashlyn grins. "Oh yeah. Thanks for the kiddie drink. I'm going to put the lights on the shrubs now." She winks at me before sauntering off.

I sip on my drink as I study Ellery. There are smudges under her eyes and brackets of strain around her mouth. She's stressed and working too hard. She needs to rest, but I have no idea how to persuade her to slow down. Especially as the inn is fully booked for the holidays.

"She's going to be the aunt who leads our child into temptation. I'm crossing her off of the approved babysitter list."

Instead of laughing at my joke, Ellery wrings her hands and avoids my gaze. Time to get to the bottom of whatever's bothering her. I place a hand on her shoulder and lead her to the porch swing.

"Sit with me while I drink my hot chocolate and have my break?" I ask but I don't wait for her to reply before gently pushing her down.

"Why do you need a break? You've been out here a whole fifteen minutes."

I shrug. "I can't let my hot chocolate get cold."

She clears her throat and I think she's going to speak, but she sighs and stares at her hands instead.

I bump her shoulder. "What's going on?"

"I-I-I have my mid-pregnancy ultrasound this week."

"What day is it?" I ask as I retrieve my phone from my pocket. "I'm free most of the week."

"Aren't you going home for Christmas?"

"Nope."

I don't tell her why because, when she discovers the reason, she's going to lose her mind, and I prefer her to lose her mind around her family since she won't lash out at me in front of them.

"It's tomorrow."

"Is there a hospital in town or do we go to the doctor? How does this all work?"

Before she can reply, Ashlyn screams, "Yes!" at the top of her lungs.

I stand and offer my hand to Ellery to help her up. "We better go check on what your sister's up to before she causes chaos."

She laughs. "Have you met Ashlyn? She's going to cause chaos no matter what we do."

"Yep. Off the approved babysitter list."

When we reach Ashlyn, she's jumping up and down. "Yes! Yes! Yes!" She sings and throws her hands in the air in victory.

"What's going on?" Ellery asks.

Ashlyn indicates the foundation. "It's here. The loot is here."

"Shush," Ellery hisses. "Do you want everyone to hear you?"

"Loot? What are you talking about?"

Ashlyn grabs my hand and drags me to the house where she points at the foundation. "Don't you see it?"

I kneel closer. "What am I supposed to be seeing?" I'm an architect. To me, this is a solid, stone foundation in an early twentieth century house, but I don't think Ashlyn's interested in my answer.

"The date. It's carved into the stone."

I study the area she indicates. "1955. What's exciting about 1955?"

"It's the year the Black Hat Bandit robbed fifty-thousand smackers from the Hastings National Bank in Nebraska."

I stand and brush the snow off my pants. "What does a robbery in 1955 have to do with Ellery's bed and breakfast?"

Before Ashlyn can answer, Ellery growls at her. "I thought we weren't telling anyone about the Mystery of the Black Hat Bandit's Missing Loot." Ashlyn whistles and avoids Ellery's gaze. "You told Rowan, didn't you?"

Ashlyn's cheeks darken. "He's a very persuasive man."

I grunt. I don't want to hear about how Rowan persuaded Ashlyn, a woman I'm beginning to think of as my little sister. "No details, please."

"I wasn't going to give you any." She wiggles her eyebrows.

Back to the matter at hand. "Let me get this straight. For some reason, you believe the money someone—"

"Not someone," she interrupts to say. "The Black Hat Bandit."

"I stand corrected. You believe the money the Black Hat Bandit robbed in Nebraska in the middle of the previous century is actually here in Winter Falls?"

"We followed the clues and it lead us here." Ashlyn gestures toward the stone.

"I think I'm going to need some whisky in my hot chocolate," I grumble.

Ellery narrows her eyes on Ashlyn. "I forbid you to dig around the area. Do you understand?" Ashlyn nods. "I need verbal confirmation."

"I promise not to go digging around," Ashlyn mumbles.

Ellery holds out her pinky. "Sister pinky swear."

Ashlyn stomps her foot and curls her bottom lip in a pout. "Do I have to?"

"Do you want me to tell Rowan about the time you followed him into the locker room—"

Ashlyn covers Ellery's mouth with her hands. "Sister pinky swear! Sister pinky swear!" They link pinkies. "I swear I won't go digging."

They drop hands and Ashlyn tramps off. "I'm getting a drink!"

"It's ten o'clock in the morning," Ellery hollers after her.

"It's five o'clock somewhere," Ashlyn shouts with a wave.

Ellery frowns down at the mess of holiday lights Ashlyn left laying in the snow. "Great. Now I need to find someone else to finish the decorating."

Is she serious? "Hello! Am I invisible? I'll do it."

Her nose scrunches up and she looks adorable. I hope our daughter resembles her. "I can't pay you much."

I cradle her face in my hands. "You're not paying me a dime. We're family. When you need help, you ask, and I'll be there."

Her green eyes sparkle up at me. "With bells on?"

I kiss the tip of her nose. "Whatever you want."

Her breath hitches and her gaze drops to my mouth. She bites her lip and I want to taste those plush lips and dive into her mouth. I won't, though. She barely agreed to stop hiding from me. If I push us past friends to lovers too quickly, she'll be the one running.

I drop my hands and step back. "Where do you want me to begin, boss?"

She frowns but her expression quickly switches to a smile. "I have the decorations all mapped out. Let me get you the instructions."

"Of course, you do," I mutter as I follow her.

I don't care if I spend the rest of the day freezing my ass off while decorating the bed and breakfast to Ellery's very specific instructions. Today is already a win. Ellery invited me to the next ultrasound without too much prodding.

And I know she still wants me as much as I want her. I don't know what I'm going to do with the information. She's not wrong when she claims I'll move back to Chicago sooner or later. But, unlike Ellery, I don't believe physical distance has to mean an end to our relationship.

Chapter Twenty

I stomp up the stairs to my parents' house for our Christmas day celebration. I'm annoyed and more than done with this conversation. The same conversation we've been having since my mid-pregnancy ultrasound yesterday.

"I am not arguing about this anymore," I grumble to Cole as I fling the door open. "I'm carrying this baby, which makes it my decision and I don't want to know the sex of the baby."

Someone gasps, and I glance over to discover a middle-aged woman standing in the center of my parent's living room. "Baby?"

I scan the area for some clue as to who this woman is and watch my sisters scurry out of the room. "Chickens!" I shout at their retreating forms.

"Bwak! Bwak!" Juniper quacks before the kitchen door swings shut behind her.

Cole grasps my hand and leads me to the woman. "Ellery West, I'd like you to meet my mother, Amy Hawkins."

I nearly stumble on my own feet at his announcement. His mother's here? No wonder he was perfectly fine staying in Winter Falls for the holidays. Because he planned to ambush me. Did my parents know about this?

I narrow my eyes on Mom, and she smiles and waves. Yep. She knew. And there goes her overnight privileges with her first grandchild. There's one advantage of bearing the first grandchild. I have blackmail material up the wazoo now.

I clear my throat and hold out my hand. "It's lovely to meet you, Mrs. Hawkins."

She ignores my hand to throw her arms around me. "It's Amy. Formality flew out the window when you announced you're having my grandchild."

I lean back to look up at her. Since she's nearly as tall as Cole, I have to lean way back. "You didn't know?"

"I was planning on surprising her," Cole answers on her behalf. "I bought her one of those cute onesies with *World's Greatest Grandma* on it."

Mom grunts. "Don't worry, Mrs. West. I bought you one, too." He winks, and I elbow him.

"Suck up."

The sliding door opens up and Dad, Lyric, and Rowan stroll inside. Dad surveys the area before sighing. "Is there a reason four of my daughters are hiding in the kitchen?"

"Not hiding, eavesdropping," Lilac clarifies because she only lies if you give her advance warning in writing – in triplicate.

"They're eavesdropping," Ashlyn shouts through the door. "I'm taste testing."

Mom growls before marching away. "Ashlyn Dream West, you better not be eating the turkey."

"Hansley," Rowan mutters under his breath causing Mom to come to a screeching halt.

Her nostrils flare as she glares up at him. Mama Bear has entered the building. Rowan is mega tall at six-feet-five while Mom is more than a foot shorter, but he still cowers under her glare. "What did you say?"

Ashlyn rushes out of the kitchen, a turkey drumstick in her hand with the rest of my sisters following her. "It's not Hansley yet. Promise."

Mom purses her lips. "You're lying."

"No, I'm not," she claims before hiding behind Rowan proving she's lying.

"When did you get married?" Mom demands to know.

"And where did you get married? And why wasn't I there? I wanted to escort my baby girl down the aisle." Dad frowns with disappointment.

"Daddy." Ashlyn rushes him and throws her arms around him. "I'm sorry. I thought since you had five daughters, you wouldn't mind missing out on one wedding. You hate Vegas anyway. Plus, I didn't want to steal the show from Aspen and Lyric."

Aspen wags her finger at Ashlyn. "Oh no, you don't. Don't throw me under the school bus and pretend it's my fault you eloped."

"Who's not surprised Ashlyn eloped?" Juniper asks as she raises her hand.

I raise my hand, too. "Wanna bet she got married by Elvis?"

"I will not accept your bet. I know baby cakes has always wanted to be married by Elvis."

Ashlyn smacks Juniper on the shoulder. "Don't you go calling me baby cakes, too. You're barely eighteen months older than me."

"Which means I have eighteen months of experience on you."

Ashlyn reaches for her again, but Rowan steps in between them. "No fighting on Christmas day."

Ashlyn flutters her lashes at him. "But it's tradition. And you're in big trouble for telling everyone we eloped."

"I didn't tell anyone."

Ashlyn cocks her hip and stares Rowan down. I count five seconds before he caves.

"It was an accident."

Mom claps her hands. "Speaking of accidents." She stands next to Cole's mom. "I'd like to introduce everyone to Amy Hawkins."

"Did you make enough food?" Ashlyn asks around a bite of turkey.

Rowan snatches the drumstick from her. "Behave, dream girl."

"I'm sorry, Mrs. Hawkins. I promise my family isn't always this crazy," I plead. This woman is the grandmother of my baby. I need her to like me.

"Liar!" Ashlyn yells, and Rowan clamps a hand over her mouth.

Mrs. Hawkins laughs. "It's fine. I always wanted a big family." Her smile dims for a moment before she forces it back. "I'm glad my grandchildren will grow up with all these aunts and uncles."

Grandchildren? I gulp. Does she think Cole and I are a couple? I glance up at him, but his expression doesn't give anything away. Great. I guess I'm navigating this minefield on my own.

"Um...well... Cole and I..."

Cole sighs. "Mom, Ellery and I aren't together."

Her eyes widen. "Oh." She clears her throat. "Even if you aren't together with my son, I'd like to think of any other children you have as my grandchildren as well." She flushes as she glances away.

I rush to her and squeeze her hands. "Of course, Mrs. Hawkins. The baby's brothers and sisters – if they ever come into being – will be as much your grandchildren as this child I'm carrying."

"Amy. We don't use last names in the family."

Her eyes water and she sniffs. Cole tucks her into his side. "Mom, you promised you wouldn't cry."

"You didn't tell me I'm going to be a grandma." She motions toward me. "You know I've always wanted ..." Her voice cuts off when she loses the battle to hold back her tears. Mom snatches her hand and escorts her away.

"Are we going to do presents first or eat first?" Lilac asks when silence falls.

"Way to be sensitive, big sis," Ashlyn mutters.

"What pray tell am I supposed to be sensitive about?" Once again, human emotions have confounded my middle sister.

"Ellery's baby grandma rushed out of here bawling her eyes out. Have a bit of care."

I throw my hands up. "No! We are not labeling Cole's mom baby grandma. And." I pause to glare at everyone. "We are also done labeling Cole baby daddy."

Ashlyn grimaces. "What about if we bought Cole a t-shirt for Christmas with baby daddy on it before you threw down this rule?"

"I'm going to kill her. Surely, a jury would understand."

Lilac clears her throat. "Unfortunately, a sibling being irritating is not a valid defense to murder."

"What if the body is never found?"

"Can you please stop talking about murdering someone in front of me," Lyric pleas.

"You're not the Chief of Police when you're in this house," Aspen says.

"I'm not? What am I then?"

"You're a member of this family. My soon-to-be husband. Speaking of which, we need to set a date. I don't approve of my baby sister getting married before me."

Ashlyn rolls her eyes. "I didn't realize there was a rule about who can get married first."

Aspen crosses her arms over her chest. "Yes, you did. You would have told someone you were eloping otherwise."

Rowan kisses Ashlyn's hair. "She's got you there."

She growls up at him. "We're supposed to be partners. You and me against the world."

"We're not the world. We're your family. And you should have told us. I've never been to Vegas. I would have loved a trip," Juniper says.

Huh. Ashlyn and Juniper are as close as Aspen and I are. I'm surprised Ashlyn didn't tell Juniper she was getting married.

"We decided spur of the moment. You wouldn't have had time to arrange someone to watch your animals."

"I could have found someone."

"Oh yeah." Ashlyn taps her cheek. "The same someone who's been phoning you constantly all day and you've been ignoring his calls?"

"Hold up. Juniper has a secret admirer, and we don't know about it?"

I shrug at Aspen's question. Between managing the inn, being pregnant, and dealing with Cole, I can barely remember my own name at the end of the day. I have zero brain space to consider Juniper's love life.

"She does," Ashlyn answers at the same time Juniper shouts, "I don't!"

Mom returns to the living room with Amy following her. She surveys the room before clapping her hands.

"You." She points to Ashlyn. "You will have a wedding reception to celebrate your marriage." She points to Juniper. "And you will you use prophylactics when you have sex with your admirer." She points to me. "And you will stop having a hissy fit every time we use the term 'baby daddy'. You should know better. Everyone's saying it because your eye twitches and you lose your mind every time."

"Once again, I am the perfect child," Lilac gloats.

"The perfect pain in my ass," Aspen mumbles.

"Did everyone forget I'm the mayor now?" Ashlyn grins. "You can't order me around anymore."

Mom pats her cheek. "Baby girl, I'm your mother. I will always have the right to order you around. Even when I'm on my death bed." Ashlyn sticks her tongue out and Mom tweaks her nose.

"Follow me. There's a ton of food to carry into the dining room. Pregnant women and their baby daddies are exempted from helping."

Everyone trudges into the kitchen leaving Cole and me alone in the living room.

"Are you certain you want to be a member of this family?" I ask as I watch Juniper trip Ashlyn.

His hand splays over my belly. "Too late now, baby mamma."

"Don't make me get out my shotgun."

He chuckles at my empty threat and his dimple comes out to play. I glance away. I will not be entranced by his dimple. I don't care if it's Christmas day and he brought his mother here to meet me. I will remain strong. Because Cole isn't from Winter Falls. He'll leave eventually. And when he does, he won't be taking my heart with him.

Chapter Twenty-One

The doorbell rings and someone knocks simultaneously. Not fair. It's New Year's Eve and the guests at the inn are all set. They should be out partying at the brewery or the bar now. No one should be knocking at my door.

There's another knock and I cover myself with the blanket. If I can't see them, they can't see me, right?

"Ellie, I know you're in there," Cole hollers through the door.

"Ellery is not here at the moment. She's not available until the new year has dawned. Please leave a message after the beep. Beep!"

"I'm coming in." He pushes through the door.

"Hey!" I drop the blanket to glare at him. "Your key is for emergencies." I know. I know. I'm the idiot who gave the man I can't have a key to my apartment. What can I say? I'm working on my advanced degree in heartbreak.

He lifts the bags he's carrying. "This is an emergency."

"Shouldn't you be out partying like it's 1999?"

"1999 was over more than two decades ago."

"It's an expression."

"Besides, I wanted to spend time with you."

Caution! Alert! Time with me? How do I respond? I know I agreed to get to know him since we're having a baby together, but I'm still reeling from Christmas and how cozy it was having him and his mom there. I have spent more hours than I care to admit daydreaming about what it would be like having him as part of my family – permanently. I don't need him digging his way into my heart any further.

The scent of fried chicken wafts toward me and my stomach rumbles. When did I last eat? Thank you, food distraction. "Did you bring my mom's fried chicken?"

"With all the fixings including coleslaw and potato salad. Plus, I picked up some chocolate chip cookies at Rowan's bakery before he closed."

"You may stay," I announce all magnanimous.

He chuckles. "I figured."

I begin to stand, but he motions for me to stay where I am. "I'll get it."

I'm too tired to argue. I plop back down on the sofa.

Cole returns and hands me a plate. "Cute pajamas."

I feel my face heat at the reminder of the flannel pajamas covered in hearts I'm wearing. They're one of the few pairs I own big enough for my belly. I really need to go shopping for pregnancy clothes.

"I wasn't expecting company."

"What are we watching?" he asks as he settles on the opposite corner of the sofa.

"*Love Actually*. Do you know it?" He shrugs. "It's one of my favorite Christmas movies."

"Push play." He motions with his fork toward the tv.

"I'll re-start it from the beginning."

Once the movie is playing, I dive into my food. When my plate is empty, I consider licking it. I wasn't kidding about being hungry.

Cole snorts as he stands and grabs my plate. "I'll get you more food before you decide to chew on the plate."

"Don't judge. I'm growing a baby here."

"I know," he growls, and the sound makes my body light up as warmth travels from my chest down to my core. Pregnancy makes you horny. True story.

He holds out another plate of food to me and I snatch it away before he can notice the blush covering me from my cheeks down my neck to my breasts. Good thing it's winter and these pajamas hide my cleavage.

When I finish my food, I place my plate on the coffee table and curl my legs underneath me. Cole snatches my feet and pulls them into his lap.

"What are you doing?"

"Relax," he says before his thumb digs into the arch of my foot.

I moan. "Oh god, that's good."

He clears his throat. "Watch the movie," he orders in a growl. I squirm as the memory of him growling while moving inside of me flashes into my head.

I do my best to pay attention to the movie, but it's difficult when Cole continues to rub my feet with those talented hands of his. He's torturing me. Two can play at this game. I inch my left foot forward until it's settled over his crotch where I discover a large bulge. A bulge I know he's as talented with as his hands.

My breasts feel heavy and my sex pulses. To hell with it. Tomorrow, I'll be responsible business owner Ellery West. Tonight, I want something for myself. I snatch my foot from Cole's hands. He raises an eyebrow in question at me.

I stand and hold out my hand to him hoping I'm not going to regret this. He places his hand in mine and intertwines our fingers before leading me to the bedroom.

Once there, he drops my hand to cradle my face. "Are you sure about this?"

I blow out a breath of air. "No, but I am afraid my body's going to go up in flames if we don't have sex this minute."

He smirks. "Go up in flames?"

"Shut it. Pregnancy hormones are no joke."

"Since I am partially to blame for those hormones, I guess I better take care of you," he says and drops to his knees.

"Yes," I hiss.

He winks up at me. "I haven't done anything yet."

I wave at him on his knees. "Get on with it then."

He grabs hold of the waistband of my pajama pants and drags the material down my legs. I step out of the pants and feel my tummy juggle. Shit. I stretch my top down over my belly and hold it there. "Um."

He bumps my hands out of the way and scrunches the shirt up under my breasts until my belly is revealed in all its glory. He lays his hands there. "You're beautiful, Ellie."

"I'm fat."

"You're not fat. You're pregnant. There's a difference. A huge difference." He winks. "But if you're unsure, say the word and we'll stop."

Instead of stopping, he trails his index finger along the edge of my panties. Back and forth. Back and forth. The motion makes me feel all needy. I squirm and try to create some friction by rubbing my thighs together.

Cole grips my thighs. "Nuh-uh. No getting yourself off. That's what I'm here for."

"But you're not doing anything," I whine.

He uses his hold to spread my thighs before his head dives between them. He runs his nose along my panties. What he doesn't do is touch me where I need him most.

That's it! I'm done with his teasing. I'm going to combust if he doesn't touch me the way I long for soon. I push him out of the way before shoving my panties down my legs. This time when my belly bounces, I ignore it. I'm too much in need to pay attention to it now.

"Someone's in a hurry," Cole complains but there's laughter in his voice.

"Someone wants to have sex before this year is over."

Cole climbs to his feet before lifting me up. I expect him to throw me onto the bed – I'm down with the plan – but he lays me gently on the bed.

"I'm not going to break."

"I know."

He slams his lips on mine and the talking is done. I immediately open and his tongue delves in. He tastes of chicken, chocolate, and sin. Three of my favorite things in the world. I thread my fingers through his hair while I wrap my legs around his hips.

He thrusts his jean clad cock into my center, and I moan down his mouth. Finally.

I wrench my mouth from his. "Jeans. Off. Now." I've forgotten how to speak in complete sentences, but Cole obviously understands as he lifts himself up to shove his jeans down his hips.

He pauses with his cock poised at my center. "Condom."

I giggle causing the head of his cock to rub against my clit. "We don't need a condom. I'm already pregnant."

"Yes, but ..."

My eyes widen and I shove at his shoulders. "Do you mean?"

He kisses my nose. "I haven't been with anyone since you, Ellie."

I nearly collapse from the relief I feel at those words. I was afraid to ask if he'd been with someone else despite being desperate to know.

"And I obviously haven't been with anyone either."

His shoulders fall in relief. "Good."

He lines his hard length up with my opening once again. "Ready?"

So ready. I use my hold on his waist to lift myself until he enters me. Finally. Cole growls before thrusting into me until he's completely seated. I arch my back as the feeling of being full hits me.

"You good?"

I smile at him. "Never better."

He gets to his knees and unwinds my legs from his waist before throwing them over his shoulders. The motion causes him to slide deeper into me.

"Are you trying to kill me?" I croak out.

He winks. "What a way to go," he says before withdrawing. I clench my inner muscles to keep him from going anywhere and he grunts.

"You keep doing that and this won't last long," he grumbles.

"And you keep on being slow as molasses and I'll have to take care of myself."

He freezes for a moment before he grins, and his dang dimple pops out. "Next time."

I bang my fist on the mattress. "There will be no next time if you—"

My words are cut off when he slams into me and pleasure rushes through me. There's no stopping him now. He thrusts in and out until sweat forms on his brow.

"You need to come for me, Ellie girl. I can't hold on much longer."

"Almost there," I grunt as I feel the warmth spread from my core to the rest of my body.

Cole reaches between us to rub circles around my clit and my body explodes.

"Cole," I squeak as my climax hits me.

I ride the wave as he continues to pound into me. Soon enough, his movements become erratic.

"Ellie," he whispers as his climax hits him. His eyes close before he throws his head back and I realize I've been staring into his eyes the entire time he's been inside me. I don't stare into my partner's eyes. I keep the lights off and the covers on.

Another piece of evidence proving I'm in way too deep with this man. I'll think about it tomorrow. When he's not pulsing inside of me. Tomorrow Ellery will deal with this problem. Today Ellery is entirely too happy. She's not letting anything ruin the afterglow.

Chapter Twenty-Two

*C*ole

I wake with my arm thrown over a warm and naked Ellery. She fell asleep after our first round of sex last night, but I woke in the middle of the night at the feel of her warm, wet mouth swallowing me.

She drove me out of my mind with pleasure using her mouth. After I came, she grinned up at me, told me she's been wanting to get her mouth on me for months, before curling up next to me and promptly falling back asleep.

I tighten my arm around the woman who's been driving me absolutely insane for the past months. I'm done fighting the pull of Ellery Promise West. She's got me ensnared and I'm not going anywhere. But I know I can't blurt out anything of the sort. She'll run away before I have the chance to put my jeans on.

She squirms in my arms. "Breakfast. I need to make breakfast."

I kiss her hair. "Shush. Get some more sleep."

She freezes. "Cole. What are you doing here?" When the memories of last night come to her, she slaps her forehead. "Ow."

I chuckle. The rest of the world sees professional Ellery West who has it together all the time. I'm the lucky bastard who gets to be there when she's not trying to be perfect. And I plan to be there with her for as long as she'll let me.

"I need to help with the breakfast service."

"No, you need to catch up on your sleep." The woman works way too hard. She needs to learn to rely on her employees more. She's not a one-woman show. She needs to stop acting like one.

"Don't you start," she grumbles. "It's my business and I'll operate it the way I want to."

"I'm not trying to tell you how to run your business. I'm trying to ensure you get enough rest. You're pregnant or have you forgotten?"

She elbows me and squirms out of my hold. "I haven't forgotten. How could I have? I'm the one who was sick every morning for months. I'm the one who can no longer fit into any of her clothes. I'm the one with all these *feelings* and hormones running rampant in my body. You haven't been here. You don't know."

Wrong thing to say. I sit up in bed and cross my arms over my chest. "I would have been here if I had known. I phoned and texted you after I had to return to Chicago. You ignored me."

She grabs her pajama top and puts it on before whirling around to glare at me. "Because I..." She trails off and throws her arms in the air.

"Because what?"

She ignores me to dig on the floor for her panties. "Forget it. It was just a one-night stand."

I throw the covers off of me and prowl to her. "I told you I wanted more than a one-night stand from the very beginning."

I'm not lying. I may have known Ellie for mere days before we fell into bed, but she fascinated me from the start with the way her eyes laughed at me when I thought she was the cleaner to how utterly sexy her curvy body is.

"I don't have time to rehash this yet again. I need to get to work."

"Moon is covering the breakfast service."

She narrows her eyes on me. "How do you know?"

Maybe because Moon covers the breakfast service every day? I keep my snide comments to myself, though. I know better than to rile this woman up any more than she already is.

"She told me." She also asked me to help convince Ellery to give her a chance to handle the breakfast service without her boss hovering over her and commenting on every single thing she does.

I try a different tactic. "It's New Year's Day. I bet all of the guests are hungover and sleeping it off."

"You're not hungover."

I smirk. "I had better things to do than tie one on last night." I lean forward and sip from her lips for a brief moment. "Happy New Year, Ellie girl."

"Happy New Year, pain in my ass Cole."

I waggle my brows. "I wasn't a pain in your ass, but I can be if you want me to."

She slaps my shoulder. "I'm going to shower and get dressed. I'll see you later."

She doesn't seriously think she's getting rid of me, does she? I let her escape into the bathroom without contradicting her. She'll figure out soon enough that I won't be as easily pushed away anymore.

I freshen up in her half-bath off of the living room before I begin working on her breakfast. I plan to surprise my girl with Rowan's famous red velvet pancakes. The pancakes are apparently how he wooed Ashlyn, although from what I've heard, she didn't need much wooing.

I'm plating the pancakes when I hear a gasp behind me. I tuck my smile away before turning around.

"What are you doing? Why are you still here?"

Ellery is dressed in her typical work clothes of black slacks and white blouse. She's ready to work another long day. It doesn't matter how today is a holiday or how she never takes a day off despite being pregnant.

I know I can't convince her to not work today. She successfully avoided my attempt at getting her to go into work later without blinking an eye. I can recognize a lost cause when I come across one. But I will force her to sit down and have a nice breakfast before she begins.

"Breakfast is served." I nod to the kitchen table I've set. "Have a seat." She doesn't move. She's probably contemplating how to kick me out without getting her white blouse dirty. She can try. I'm not leaving.

I lift the plate of pancakes. "Or do you want these to get cold?"

She inches closer. "What are these?"

I smirk. "Only Rowan's red velvet pancakes."

Her eyes widen. "Rowan was here?"

"No, silly. I made them."

"Rowan gave you his red velvet pancake recipe? I don't believe you."

"What? Is it a closely guarded secret?" I ask despite knowing it is. Rowan described in extremely graphic detail what he'd do to me if the recipe became public knowledge. I have no plans to tell anyone the recipe. I like the skin on my balls where it is.

I set the plate of pancakes on the table before guiding a shocked Ellie to the table. "Do you want your one cup of coffee now or later?"

"My one cup of coffee?"

"You can't have too much caffeine when you're pregnant."

She frowns. "I'll have milk, please."

I pour her a glass of milk before joining her at the table. There isn't much room, and my legs press against hers.

Ellery bites into her pancake and her eyes shut before she groans. "Now I know why Rowan refuses to give the recipe away."

I'm not usually the jealous type, but hearing my girl say another man's name while she groans pisses me off. "I'm the one who slaved over the oven to make the pancakes."

She pats my hand. "Of course, you did."

My jealousy vanishes at her mothering me. "You're going to be a great mother."

Her nose wrinkles. "I don't know. I have no idea what I'm doing."

"Said by every parent in the world at least a thousand times a day."

"And I work all the time. How can I be a good parent when I'll never see my child?"

"You have plenty of support around you. I know your mom is eager to babysit."

She snorts. "And spoil the child."

"It's a grandmother's privilege or so my mom's told me about a gazillion times since she found out she's going to be a grandma."

Mom got over her shock of becoming a grandmother in approximately two point eight seconds. She fell in love with Ellery and the West family five seconds later. She's planning to return to Winter Falls for Easter. She was completely charmed by the town. She couldn't stop talking about how great a place it would be to grow up. I won't be surprised if she wants to move here.

I'm not there yet. My plan is to convince Ellery to move. I don't know how since her business is here and you can't exactly pick the inn up and place it in another location, but maybe I can find another old property for her to renovate for a bed and breakfast. In Chicago. Near me. Between my architectural skills and her knowledge of hostelry, the possibilities are endless.

"And I'm not prepared," Ellery whines and brings me back to the room. "I don't have a crib or baby clothes or..." She throws her hands in the air. "I don't even know what stuff I need."

"We'll figure it out."

She doesn't hear me as she continues to rant. "And look at me. I'm wearing my blouses untucked because I haven't bought pregnancy clothes yet. What woman who's five months pregnant hasn't bought pregnancy clothes yet?"

I grasp her hand. "You're barely showing."

"Did you not notice the humongous belly I have last night?"

Oh, I noticed. It isn't humongous, but it is gorgeous. Watching her belly grow as my child develops inside of her is a major turn-on. I can't wait to watch as her belly swells even more in the coming months.

"Humongous is a bit of an exaggeration."

She wags her fork at me. "Don't tell me I'm exaggerating!"

I hold my hands up in surrender. "I rescind my comment." I indicate her plate. "Now, eat your pancakes before they get cold. Rowan will never give me a recipe again if you don't appreciate his pancakes."

She grunts before diving into her food. As she eats, I begin to formulate my plan. A plan to convince Ellery I'm the man for her. Because I am the man for her. I know it. She just needs to figure it out.

Chapter Twenty-Three

I sigh as I sink into my chair in my office. I make sure the door is closed before unbuttoning my pants. Truth be told, it's not a button situation anymore. I'm using an elastic band to keep my pants together. I really need to move buying pregnancy pants up on my to-do list, but who has the time?

The door opens and I sit up before my visitor notices my pants situation. I puff out a breath in relief when I see it's just Cole. Just Cole? There's nothing 'just' about the man.

He smirks before stalking toward me like he's the predator and I'm his prey. Oh my. Is it hot in here? His blue eyes sparkle and his dark hair is all messed up as if he's been running his hands through it non-stop. It's my job to run my hands through his hair and ruin his hairdo.

Wait a minute, Ellery. It's not your job. Nothing to do with Cole is *your* anything except raising this baby together. And having sweaty fun between the sheets. Nope. No more sex. I needed to scratch an itch is all. But somehow the itch got worse after I scratched it. Oh boy.

"C-c-can I help you?" Great. Now, I'm stuttering.

Cole doesn't stop until he's looming over me. I lean back in my chair to gaze up at him. Are architects supposed to be this sexy?

Shouldn't he be a skinny nerd with white pasty skin from being inside all the time? Not a bronze skinned beauty with broad shoulders.

He kisses my forehead. "I've got a surprise for you."

I ignore how his lips on my skin make me feel and concentrate on his words. "A surprise?"

"Yep." He grasps my hands and heaves me from my chair.

I whirl around to fix my pants before they fall to my knees. Although if my pants were around my knees, it would give Cole easy access to my core which started pulsing the second I laid eyes on the man. *Knock it off, Ellery.* You're not a sex-craved kitten. You don't even like kittens, remember?

"Are we going somewhere?" I ask once I'm presentable again.

"We are," he says and hauls me out of my office.

"Where to?"

"It's a surprise," he murmurs as he guides me out of the inn and into the parking lot toward his Jeep.

"Did you get a dispensation to drive your car in Winter Falls?"

He opens the door and helps me into the passenger seat before responding, "As a matter of fact, I did."

My mouth drops open, and he tweaks my nose before shutting the door and rounding the front of the vehicle. He hops in and switches on the engine. When he turns left out of the parking lot, I realize we're leaving Winter Falls.

"Where are we going?"

"It's a surprise."

Ugh. Enough with repeating 'it's a surprise'.

"It's a surprise as in you're going to tie me up and kidnap me?"

His gaze whips to mine and the jeep swerves. He clears his throat and returns his attention to the road. "Do you want me to tie you up?"

I was kidding, but now I'm thinking about him tying me up and blindfolding me while I'm naked and he explores every inch of my skin. I rub my thighs together to create a bit of friction as the fantasy causes my body to heat and tingles to erupt in my core.

"I think you're fond of the idea. I'm all for experimenting the next time we're in bed."

The next time we're in bed? Whoa, Ellie! Cole and I aren't in a relationship. Well... We are in a relationship. A relationship as in co-parenting our baby-to-be. Not a relationship as in we're a couple. Cole's an out-of-towner, remember?

"I don't think we should add sex to our relationship."

Cole frowns over at me. "You seemed to think it was a wonderful idea the other day."

Yes, because I was horny and feeling lonely at being by myself on New Year's Eve.

"It was a mistake."

"Didn't feel like a mistake to me," he mutters before raising his voice, "But let's not talk about it today."

"What are we doing today?"

He laughs. "Nice try, but I'm not telling."

Glad to have dodged the bullet of discussing our non-relationship, I decide to move the conversation along. "How is the community center project going?"

"I'm working on getting all of the proper planning permissions before we can begin. On a related note, are we certain your sister Lilac is human and not a robot?"

I giggle. "No, we're not. Mom claims there's decisive proof, but I don't believe her. Pictures can be manipulated."

"How is it possible for one person to have memorized every single town ordinance as well as all the state and federal laws?"

Our conversation continues on this light note as we drive thirty minutes to an outlet mall. "We're going shopping?" I ask as Cole parks the Jeep.

"We are." He nods to the store in front of us – *Baby and Me*.

Hold on. He took me to a baby store?

When I don't respond, he backpedals. "I'm sorry. Would you prefer to shop for pregnancy clothes with your sisters? I don't have siblings. I didn't think."

"Shut up," I hiss. Tears well in my eyes and spill over my lashes down my cheeks. "I can't believe you brought me here."

Cole's out of the vehicle and around to my side in a flash. He flings open the door and pulls me into his arms.

"Shush, baby. I'm sorry. I'll drive you home. Or I'll call your sisters to meet you here. Whatever you want. But, please, stop crying. I can't handle your tears."

"It's your fault for being so sweet," I mumble into his shirt, which is now wet from my tears and snot. A pretty crier I am not.

He palms my neck before leaning down until we're eye to eye. "You're not upset with me?"

I slap at his shoulders. "No, you jerk."

He chuckles as his fingers wipe away my tears. "I believe the term is sweet jerk."

"Stop being nice."

He steps back. "Fine. Get your ass into the store. We're not leaving until you have an entire new wardrobe."

"I can't afford a new wardrobe," I mumble as he helps me out.

"You're not paying."

"Whatever." I am paying, but I'm not arguing about it while standing in a parking lot with a blotchy face from having a crying jag.

Cole places his hand on my lower back and escorts me into the store. I expect him to skedaddle as soon as I'm inside, but he leads me to the clothing section. Once there, he points to the cribs.

"I'll be over there if you need me."

"You're not buying a crib," I shout after him.

"Honey," a woman across from me says and I startle, "if the man wants to buy you a crib, let him buy you a crib."

"But I—"

"Hush now. Are you carrying his baby?" I nod. "Let him buy you a crib," she says before sauntering off. And I thought nosiness was limited to the people of Winter Falls. Guess not.

I pick out a few pairs of pants and some blouses to try on and make my way to the dressing rooms. I hang up the clothes and begin removing my pants. I squeal and try to cover myself when the door opens behind me.

"It's me," Cole says as he sits on the chair in the corner of the room. "Let's see what you've got."

"You can't be in here," I hiss.

"No one's going to know. There aren't any cameras in here."

"I do know," someone shouts from outside, "but you're fine in there as long as there's no hanky-panky."

Cole grins up at me. "Told you."

"Maybe I don't want you seeing me naked."

"Ellie girl, that ship has sailed."

"Whatever." I whirl around to try on my pants without looking at his stupid, gorgeous face.

"These pants are great. How do they feel? Is there room for baby to grow in them?"

I drop my chin to my chest. Great. It's not bad enough he's in here with me, he's also going to comment on all my clothes?

"They're fine."

And so it goes. I try on an item and Cole comments because keeping his mouth shut is apparently impossible.

"I'm done," I claim after I've tried on the last blouse.

He frowns. "You only have two pairs of pants and two blouses in the yes pile."

I shrug. "I don't need any more."

"Okay." He stands. "Get dressed. We'll grab some lunch before we head home."

Home? Winter Falls isn't his home. Before I have a chance to correct him, he's strolling out of the dressing room with all the clothes in his hands.

When I exit a few minutes later, Cole's already at the cash register. He lifts up a bag and smiles when he notices me. "We're all set."

"I told you I was going to pay for the clothes. They're my clothes after all."

"I was already cashing out since I needed to pay for a few other items."

I narrow my eyes on him. "What other items?"

He claims my hand and directs me out of the store. "Did you want to eat at the hamburger joint we passed on the way here? Ashlyn claims the burgers there are to die for."

"Are you going to answer my question?"

"No."

"No?" I screech.

"My answer will make you mad, so no."

"I'm already mad," I growl. The man is infuriating.

He sighs. "Hop in the jeep and I'll fill you in on the way to lunch."

Once we're on our way, I ask again, "What other items?"

"A crib, a changing table, a diaper pail, a baby monitor."

"What the hell, Cole? That's everything I need for the baby's nursery."

"Not everything. You still need a rocking chair or glider, but I wasn't certain which one you'd want. I figure you can pick one out later."

"You've lost your mind. Truly lost your mind. Where am I going to put everything? I don't have room for a big nursery in my place. I figured I'd put a crib in my bedroom."

He clears his throat. "Actually."

"Oh, for crying out loud, what now?"

"You do remember I'm an architect."

"Yes." I nod. "You think it's fun to play with crayons."

"I do. I also think it's fun to draw buildings and such."

"Spit it out. What did you do?"

"I came up with a way to build a nursery in your apartment."

"What?" My eyes nearly bug out of my head. "How? Where?"

"We'll need to move some of the walls, but you have enough space."

Move the walls? I hold up my hand. "Stop talking. I can't with you anymore."

I'm not lying. I can't handle him coming up with yet another way to help me. He's being sweet and acting as if he's going to be in my life forever. Something I know to not be true. I can't get used to him being here. I'll be devastated when he's gone.

Oh, who am I kidding? I'll be devastated when he's gone no matter what. No matter how much I've tried to sever the string tethering us together, it's only getting stronger.

Chapter Twenty-Four

"I don't know why we have to go shopping for your wedding dress when you haven't picked a date yet," I grump as we enter the wedding boutique.

"Because I want a fairytale wedding," Aspen sings as she spins around.

"I didn't need a fairytale wedding." Ashlyn wiggles her left hand at everyone. Since Rowan spilled the beans about them eloping, she's been wearing a diamond encrusted wedding band to match her diamond engagement ring.

"Were you ever going to tell us you're married?" I don't know how she managed to keep the news to herself.

"We planned a big reveal on Valentine's Day. Rowan was going to make a cake announcing Mr. and Mrs. Hansley to the world."

"I want one of those tiered wedding cakes. Enough to feed the entire town," Aspen says as she glides past us.

Lilac frowns. "I don't think you're supposed to be dancing in a store."

"I'm the bride. I can do whatever I want."

"Let's get this show on the road." Juniper taps her watch. "I need to get back to my animals."

"What a shocker." Ashlyn rolls her eyes. "Juniper prefers to be with her animals than her family."

Juniper's phone rings and she hurries to switch it off without bothering to check who's calling.

Aspen rushes to her. "Is it your secret admirer? Pick up the phone! We can listen in and give you tips."

"Tips?" I snort. "You're going give tips on love? You're marrying your childhood sweetheart. You're not qualified."

Ashlyn raises her hand and waves it to and fro making sure her wedding rings sparkle. The rings probably weigh more than her hand. There's no need to shove them in our faces. "Am I qualified? I am the only sister who's married after all."

"Ms. West?" A woman enters the reception area. "We're ready for you now."

"This place is fancy. Exactly how much money is Aspen planning to spend on a wedding gown?" Juniper mutters as we follow Aspen.

Fancy is right. The room we walk into is something out of a movie. There are several plush sofas arranged around a small, round elevated stage. I wonder if it revolves. Next to the sofas are accent tables with trays of small sandwiches and glasses of champagne laid out on them.

"Not it," Ashlyn shouts as she dives on the champagne.

Lilac picks up a glass as well. "There's no reason to yell not it. Ellery is our designated driver." Her gaze dips to my stomach. "Obviously."

"Glad to be of service," I mumble before collapsing on the sofa. Lilac and Juniper join me while Aspen stands with the sales lady and Ashlyn rushes around the room touching every single dress with her grubby hands.

"My name is Brooke and I'll be assisting you with all your bridal needs today," the sales lady begins. "Do you know what type of wedding dress you prefer?"

Aspen bobs her head. "Yes. I want a ballgown."

"You might as well show her the clippings. It'll make things easier," I say because I know Aspen's been collecting ideas for her wedding dress since she was sixteen and Lyric told her he loved her for the first time. I would know. I shared a bedroom with her, and she wouldn't shut up about how she was going to marry him until she left for college.

"I might have a few ideas." Aspen removes a book from her purse and hands it to Brooke.

Ashlyn plops down on the sofa across from me. "This place is super chic." She grabs the plate of sandwiches. "Who's hungry?" She doesn't wait for anyone to answer before she stuffs a sandwich in her face.

Lilac consults her watch. "It's not yet noon. Didn't you eat breakfast?"

Ashlyn shrugs. "It was a long time ago. This is second breakfast. Or is it elevenses?"

"We're not in a fantasy novel. Neither second breakfast nor elevenses exist in real life," Lilac claims.

"Who says?"

Lilac doesn't respond to Ashlyn's sarcastic tone and merely tells her, "all of society."

"Uh oh." Ashlyn elbows me. "She put on her social scientist hat."

Lilac frowns. "Social studies is not a science."

"If you can get a degree in it, it's a science," Juniper declares.

Aspen returns and sits on the stage in front of us. "Brooke is going to find some gowns for me to try on."

JUST FOR FOREVER 161

"Here." Ashlyn hands her a glass of champagne before raising her own. "To Aspen and Lyric getting married."

"Finally," Aspen murmurs as she clinks her glass with Ashlyn's.

"Are you planning for all four of us to be your bridesmaids? And who's your maid of honor?" Ashlyn asks.

"Don't be silly. You know Ellery will be her maid of honor. And Mom will kill her if we're not all bridesmaids."

I'm surprised at Juniper's declaration. I haven't given a thought to being Aspen's maid of honor. I survey my stomach. "When exactly are you planning to get married?" Parading down the aisle with a tummy as big as a beach ball in a church while being unwed is asking for trouble of the cosmic variety.

Ashlyn elbows me. "She hasn't set a date yet, remember? Is pregnancy brain a thing? Do you become forgetful?"

"You'll find out soon enough." I nod toward her glass of champagne. "Although..."

She sniffs. "Yeah. No pregnancy this month for me."

Juniper throws an arm around her. "Don't worry, little sis. It'll happen. You have time."

"But I want to give Rowan everything he wants, and he wants a family."

I roll my eyes. "You don't have to give him *everything* he wants."

Aspen shifts closer. "What do you mean?"

Oh crap. Have I given myself away? Is bloodhound Aspen on the case? I lean back. "Nothing. Except a woman shouldn't change herself to be with a man."

"I'm not—"

Aspen shoves her palm in Ashlyn's face. "Quiet. We're working on Ellery's problems now."

"I don't have a problem."

Her gaze lowers to my belly and she lifts an eyebrow.

I lay my hands over my bump. "Don't you dare call my baby a problem," I hiss at her.

"I'm not. I'm referring to your problem with the baby da— The child's father," she corrects before I can lash out at her.

"I don't have a problem with Cole." Except for wanting him to do wicked things to me constantly. I'm blaming the pregnancy hormones. They make me want to have sex all the time. It's not my fault they've honed in on Cole.

Aspen's finger circles my face. "Is everyone seeing what I'm seeing?"

Lilac nods. "Yes. She's blushing and her pulse rate has increased."

"Meaning …"

"Meaning she's either having a hot flash or she's turned on."

"We're in a bridal salon. I'm not turned on," I snarl at Lilac.

She shrugs. "I'm merely stating the facts."

"I can't be blushing because I'm hot?"

"The temperature in here is a perfect sixty-eight degrees. If you're warm, we should return to my hot flash hypothesis."

"How do you know it's sixty-eight degrees in here?" Ashlyn doesn't wait for her to answer and hurries off to search for the thermometer. "Holy balls! She's right. It is sixty-eight degrees in here."

"Can you figure out the exact temperature with your tongue? Can you teach me?" Juniper asks. "I'm constantly using a thermometer to check the temp of the milk when I feed the baby animals. It'd be super handy if I didn't need a thermometer all the time."

"Who cares about your animals?" Ashlyn shoves Juniper. "This is a cool party trick." She rubs her hands together. "Imagine all the bets we could win."

Lilac purses her lips. "I can't determine the temperature in the room with my tongue or by any other means. I noticed the thermometer when we entered."

"Oh." Ashlyn's shoulders hunch before she shrugs it off and grabs another glass of champagne.

"I think you're supposed to limit yourself to one glass," Juniper scolds her.

"This is Ellery's glass."

Aspen kneels in front of me and studies my face. I rear back. "What are you doing?"

"I'm trying to figure out if you've had sex."

I wave a hand over my belly. "Obviously."

"I mean recently." Her nose wrinkles as she studies me. I clear my throat and glance away. "Aha! She has had sex recently."

"You're schlepping Cole?" Ashlyn asks. "I thought you were 'just friends'." She makes air quotes but forgets she's holding a glass and nearly drops the thing. As it is, she spills the bubbly on her sweater, which she then proceeds to lick off. My baby sister is a class act.

"I am not schlepping Cole."

"Survey says," Aspen makes a buzzer noise, "Ellery's a big, fat liar who's sleeping with her baby daddy."

"Will you keep it down?" I hush her.

"Why? We're alone in here. I made an appointment and everything."

"Exactly. We're here to help you pick out a wedding dress." I motion to the sales lady who has impeccable timing and is at this very moment returning to the room towing a rack of dresses with her.

Aspen bounces to her feet and claps. "Wedding dresses! I'm marrying Lyric." She skips off to peruse the dresses, but before she reaches the rack, she spins around and points at me. "But we're not done discussing this."

Oh, yes, we are. I am not discussing having sex with Cole with my sister who is disgustingly in love with the same man she's been in love with forever. A man who's from Winter Falls and won't ever leave. A man who would never cheat on her because he's besotted with her.

I sound jealous, but I'm not. Not exactly. Until a few months ago, a man wasn't on my radar at all. Managing the inn keeps me busy. I don't have time for a man. I caress my belly. I don't exactly have time for a baby either, but I've got no choice. He's on his way whether I'm prepared or not.

And – thanks to Cole overriding my objections – I'm more prepared now than I was mere days ago. He drafted plans to create a nursery in my apartment, and he bought nearly every piece of furniture I need. He's jumping into fatherhood with two feet. Too bad I can't trust him to jump into a relationship with me with both feet.

Chapter Twenty-Five

I collapse in the chair at my office and contemplate crawling underneath it for a nap. I could steal a pillow and blanket from the supply closet and make it a cozy, little retreat. Oh, who am I kidding? Crawling is now beyond my capabilities.

I set my phone on the desk and notice a cup I didn't put there. I lift it and sniff. Peppermint tea. Yum. My phone buzzes with a message and I glance over to read it.

Drink your tea.

Cole strikes again! Since we had sex on New Year's Eve, he's been Mr. Sweet and Supportive. I can't handle him being sweet especially not with these pregnancy hormones rolling around in my body. They want to jump him before turning into a stage 4 clinger and never letting him go. Not happening.

I send him a text thanking him for the tea. I may not want to want him, but I'm not a complete bitch. I sip my tea while I work on the reservations for the Imbolc celebration, the first weekend of February. It's not as easy as it sounds. Not when the twenty reservations are accompanied by forty different room requests. I wish I were exaggerating.

The door creaks open and I glance up to find Cole standing there. "Let's go," he says and holds his hand out.

I squint at his hand. "Let's go where? Where are we going? It better not be another shopping trip."

He totally pulled one over on me there. Not only did he buy all the necessities for the baby's nursery, but he bought me a mound of pregnancy clothes. I don't need ten pairs of pants! But try to tell Cole that. The man specializes in selective hearing.

"No shopping. We're going for a walk."

I check the clock. "It's the middle of the work day."

"It's always the middle of the work day for you," he mumbles before clearing his throat. "Taking walks is good for you."

I frown. "Have you been reading pregnancy books?"

He shoves his hands in his pockets and rocks back on his feet while he shrugs. "Maybe?"

Dang it! This is exactly what I mean. He's too sweet for his own good.

"I'd rather have a nap," I say as I stand and approach him.

"I can escort you to your apartment."

I snort. "I don't need an escort to my apartment, which is basically in the backyard."

He places a finger over my mouth. "I wasn't finished." Finished? What's he talking about? When he touches me, I forget words exist. I step back and his hand drops.

"Finished?"

"I can escort you to your apartment in the backyard and stand guard over you to make sure no one bothers you for thirty minutes if you want to have a nap."

"Stand guard? What am I? The Queen of England?"

His eyes dip to my stomach, which seems to be growing with every second. "Nope. She's no longer of child rearing age. What you are is a workaholic who allows everyone to bother her."

"What?"

He shepherds me out the backdoor and into the parking lot while I seethe. I do not *let* everyone bother me. I'm the boss. I make all the final decisions. Of course, everyone comes to me with questions. It's natural.

He whirls me around and cradles my face. "Take a breath."

My nostrils flare. "I'll take a breath when I want to!"

"Ellie girl, I wasn't trying to make you mad."

"Congratulations! You did anyway." Somewhere in the back of my mind – way, way in the back of my mind – I realize I sound like a petulant child, but I couldn't care less at the moment.

"I only mean you work too hard and deserve to have time for yourself."

I shove his hands away. "There is nothing wrong with working hard."

He lifts his hands in surrender. "I didn't say there was."

I fist my hands on my hips. "Sure sounded like it."

"I'm trying to ensure you get enough rest."

"You're not my mother."

He prowls toward me, and I back up until I'm plastered to the door with him caving me in. "Damn straight, I'm not your mother. Would your mother do this?"

His lips slam down on mine and pleasure blasts through me as his taste coats my tongue. I suck on his tongue, and he moans down my throat. The vibration makes me lose control. I grab hold of his shoulders and pull him close until my breasts are squished between us.

Cole squeezes my ass and lifts until I wrap my legs around him. And then we're moving. Except unlike in a movie, we slam into a car and the alarm blares to notify the entire town what we're up to.

I wrench my lips from his and gulp air into my lungs. "We can't do this."

He punches his hips, and I feel his hard length press against my core. "We can. And, as I recall, we're pretty spectacular at it."

I bite my lip as I contemplate throwing caution into the wind. Who am I kidding? I wouldn't be throwing caution to the wind, I'd be burning the sucker down.

I scan the parking lot as I try to get my mind to go back online and be helpful instead of letting my hormones override my thinking. My gaze lands on Cole's jeep and I notice the Illinois license plate. That'll do it. My mind is firmly back online.

I push on his shoulders. "Let me down."

He doesn't hesitate to set me on my feet. He makes sure I'm steady before retreating a step. "What happened? Where did you go?"

"I didn't go anywhere. I'm right here." Except I'm staring at the ground and refusing to look him in the eye like I'm a big, fat chicken.

He places a finger under my chin and lifts until we're eye to eye. "Ellie girl, I'm not an idiot. Please don't lie to me."

I stare at him for a long time as I consider how to respond. I can brush him off again, but is that fair? He's been forthcoming about his wish to move our relationship from co-parents to lovers. I should be honest with him.

I clear my throat. "We need to talk."

To Cole's credit, he doesn't flinch at my declaration despite everyone in the world knowing 'we need to talk' is code for 'you are not going to be happy with what I have to say'.

"Let's go to my apartment."

He places his hand on my lower back and guides me toward the carriage house. As we walk, I reconsider. It's bad enough my sisters know what a fool I was about Bob. I don't need this man knowing, too.

We reach my apartment and settle in on opposite ends of the sofa. I wring my hands as I try to figure out where to begin or come up with a lie he'll buy.

"Shall I make us some tea?"

I groan. "No. You can't be sweet now."

He smirks. "What can I say? I'm a sweet guy."

I roll my eyes. "Goofball."

Silence falls and it's the awkward type that makes you want to blurt out the first thing to pop into your mind, which is what I do.

"I don't trust out-of-towners."

He chuckles. "I hate to tell you this, Ellie, but this is not a surprise."

"I can't be in a relationship with you, because I don't trust you not to cheat on me when you're not here."

He growls. "You think I'll cheat on you?"

"You don't get it."

"Damn straight, I don't. Explain it to me."

"When I was in college I fell in love with a man, Bob, he left and moved to Seattle where he lived with another woman while still being in a long-distance relationship with me."

I glance over at Cole, expecting to witness understanding on his face but am instead confronted with anger. A muscle in his cheek jerks as he clenches his jaw. The waves of fury rolling off of him are practically visible.

"Are you mad?" I ask like a complete idiot. Of course, he's mad. "Why are you mad?"

"Are you kidding me?" The question bursts out of him. "You basically told me you will never trust me because of what some asshat in college did to you. I," he slams his fist against his chest, "am a thirty-four-year-old man. I am not an asshole kid whose only thought is getting his dick wet."

I flinch at the venom spewing forth from his mouth. "But you don't live here. Once the community center project is finished, you'll be gone. Don't you get it? I can't leave Winter Falls. My entire life is here. My family and friends, my business. I've spent the last ten years of my life building my business. A business, may I remind you, that I cannot move. Literally. The *Inn on Main* will always be on Main Street."

His anger seeps out of him. "And you'll never move away?"

"No. Sorry. I won't move away." I rub my belly. "Especially not with baby West on the way."

"Baby Hawkins," he corrects.

"Whatever the baby's last name is doesn't matter." I slam the lid shut on the can of worms labeled baby's last name. "What matters is I want my baby to grow up here in Winter Falls where it's safe and every single person in town will watch out for him."

"I can't change your mind?"

"I'm sorry, Cole, but no. On this, I'm firm."

He inhales a deep breath before climbing to his feet. "Okay. Thank you for telling me," he says before walking out the door and, I fear, my life.

I swipe the tears away as they fall. It had to be done. No matter how much I may want Cole in my life. My life is here. His isn't. The end.

Chapter Twenty-Six

> **Get your bottom off the sofa and get over here.**

Tonight is the monthly book club at Aspen's bookstore, but I have no intention of abandoning my sofa anytime soon. She can send as many messages as she wants. I'm not moving. I'm exhausted from work.

I'm also a liar.

I'm always exhausted from work. My refusal to go anywhere has nothing to do with my exhaustion and everything to do with my heart hurting. No matter how much I told myself not to fall for Cole, my heart didn't listen. I rub a hand over my chest before replying to Aspen's text.

> **I don't wanna.**

Even in text form, my words sound whiny. Probably because I'm feeling whiny. I haven't heard a word from Cole since yesterday when I told him about Bob and explained how I will never move away from Winter Falls.

I know he's still checked in at the inn, but he must be avoiding me because I haven't seen him. Apparently, he's better at hiding from me than I am from him because I haven't been able to catch a glimpse of him since he walked out of my apartment.

This is how it has to be, Ellery. I know. I know. It doesn't mean it doesn't hurt, though. And holy shit balls does it hurt.

> **I'm not feeling well.**

Yep. I've resorted to outright lying to my family. When needs must.

"You don't look ill to me," Ashlyn shouts through the door before strolling inside like she owns the place. Contrary to what she thinks, she is not welcome anywhere she shows up.

"Hey! My door was locked."

"Why are you surprised every time I open a locked door? You should really know better by now."

"I'm tired. I need rest."

She grasps my hand and pulls me to my feet. "What you need is to be around your friends and family."

I narrow my eyes on her. Why does she think I need comfort? What does she know?

"You're growing my niece—"

"Or nephew," I interrupt to say because I really want a little boy who resembles Cole with his blue eyes and dark, curly hair.

Ashlyn inclines her head. "Or nephew. Whatever. We – your family – are here for you. We know it can't be easy being pregnant on your own. The point is. You're not alone." She claps her hands. "Get changed. Time to go."

I rush her and throw my arms around her. "Thanks, baby cakes."

She pats my back. "You're welcome, but I will get you to stop calling me baby cakes if it's the last thing I do."

I laugh as I walk to my bedroom to get changed. "You'll be old and gray, and we'll still call you baby cakes."

Fifteen minutes later we enter *Fall Into A Good Book*. Feather, Petal, Sage, Cayenne, and Clove cheer.

"Finally!" Feather shouts.

"Now, we can begin," Sage adds.

"I hate to break it to you, but I didn't read the book this month. You didn't need to wait for me."

"We're not here to discuss the book," Cayenne says.

"We're not?" Lilac slams her e-reader closed. "Why did I read this book if we're not going to discuss it?"

"Didn't you enjoy the book, Lilac?" Ashlyn asks.

Lilac purses her lips. "Don't act all high and mighty with me. I know you didn't read it either."

Before Ashlyn can respond with whatever lie she's planning to tell us, a dog growls and another dog barks before the two of them crash through the baby gate behind the cash register and rush to Juniper who drops to her knees.

"What's wrong with my babies? Were you feeling trapped by the inhumane baby gate?" She scratches them behind the ears and kisses their snouts.

"Ew." Ashlyn feigns gagging. "Do you kiss your man with that mouth?"

"I don't have a man."

"What about the secret admirer?" Lilac asks.

"Wait a doggone minute! Juniper Berry West has a secret admirer?" Sage asks. "I do not believe it. If I don't know about it, it can't be true."

I snort. Sage thinks being the police dispatcher means she knows everybody's secrets. She didn't know mine.

"You don't know everything going on in this town, Sage. You didn't know I was pregnant, did you?"

"Of course, we did!"

I shake my head. "I mean before my sisters found out."

"We knew," Cayenne claims.

I cross my arms over my chest and tap my toe. "You did? You all knew? Yet you said nothing and told no one?" I'm not buying it.

"We weren't sure if Cole was the father, which is why we tried hurrying Lilac along with reviewing the bids for the community center," Sage claims.

Lilac sighs. "It's true. They tried meddling in the review."

"And now we know Cole's the father," Sage proclaims.

"What we don't know is how Cole is in the sack," Feather says.

"Yeah, Ellery, how's Cole in the sack?" Petal asks.

"Nope. I'm not doing this. If Ashlyn can keep her sex life private, I can, too."

Ashlyn startles at the sound of her name and glances up from her e-reader. "Leave me out of this."

Indiana Bones barks in agreement, and I seize the chance to change the topic of conversation. "Why did you bring your dogs, Juniper?"

"Bark Twain is sick. I couldn't leave him behind at home, and Indiana Bones insisted on coming with."

"Where's Waffles?"

Aspen frowns. "You mean the owner of this establishment's dog? The dog who belongs here? I had to ask Lyric to bring him home since these two don't play nice."

"Hey!" Juniper covers her dogs' ears with her hands. "You'll hurt their feelings."

While everyone's distracted by Juniper and Aspen's argument, I collapse in the chair next to Ashlyn.

"No time to finish the book this month?"

"Between managing the recording studio and narrating my audiobook assignments, I've been busy."

I nudge her. "And you haven't been busy trying to make a baby?"

She waggles her eyebrows. "It's not a chore."

Considering Rowan is a six-foot-five former professional football player, I'm positive it isn't. Although Cole wasn't a professional athlete and yet his ability to use his body to bring mine pleasure is unparalleled. I fan my face as I imagine him above me, thrusting into me.

Ashlyn studies my face. "What are you thinking about?"

"I'm thinking pregnancy hormones are no joke."

She sighs. "I wouldn't know."

I bump her shoulder. "You can't expect to get pregnant on the first try."

"You did."

I rub my hands over my belly. "Yeah, but I'm an overachiever."

She giggles. "True."

"It'll work out and, if it doesn't, you'll make it work out." Because my sister doesn't let anything stand in her way when she has a goal. She was in love with Rowan for years before he noticed she was more than an annoying little sister of a friend. Yet she never gave up on him.

Not like Cole gave up on me. I told him I would never move and why and boom! he's done with me. I stare down at my growing belly. I hope he's not done with our child, although he did promise he would never abandon his child. Considering his reasons, I believe him.

Still. I should have stuck to my plan. Work hard at making the inn one of the premier bed and breakfasts in the state and country. Men and relationships do nothing but complicate things and get in the way of you achieving your goals.

Ashlyn squeezes my hand. "What about you? Will things work out with you?"

I smile her way, but it's forced. "When did my baby sister get this smart?"

"I've always been this smart. But my intelligence might have been hidden under my troublemaker exterior."

I snort. "You think?"

"I can't help it. Trouble finds me even when I'm not looking for it."

"In other words, you sometimes go searching for it."

She winks. "What's life without a little trouble?"

"I wouldn't know. I'm not a troublemaker."

"Really? You didn't skip school?"

I roll my eyes. I skipped school a total of two times in my life. "You're seriously comparing skipping school to terrorizing the librarian?"

She shrugs. "How could I know Gratitude believes in ghosts?"

Aspen clears her throat. "If we could begin tonight's discussion of …" She checks the cover of the book she's holding. "*Midnight Train to Happy.*"

I can't help the laugh from escaping. Who comes up with these books?

"There's nothing wrong with a guilty pleasure read," Feather shouts.

"I agree, but it would be nice if we could read something a bit more intellectual," Aspen suggests.

"I have a list I can recommend," Lilac says before unlocking her phone. "*Sapiens, a brief history of mankind, A Brief History of Time—*"

"Thank you, Lilac. We'll add those books to our potential future reads."

"I'll email you the list," Lilac responds. Aspen laughs, and she frowns. "You were being sarcastic, weren't you?"

As I laugh at poor Lilac's inability to understand sarcasm, I realize Ashlyn was right. It is good to be surrounded by friends and family. At the very least, this so-called book club meeting will help get my mind off Cole walking away from me for a few minutes.

Chapter Twenty-Seven

Cole

I pace my room as I consider what I've done. Or, I guess I should say, what I'm about to do. I pause to rip the letter from the printer. I fist the piece of paper in my hand as I consider yet again if I'm doing the right thing.

But there's actually nothing left to deliberate. I'm done considering. Done weighing both sides of the coin. It's done. The decision is made. I won't let my family slip from my fingers. I am not my father. A man who doesn't deserve the designation of 'father'.

I leave my room and bound down the stairs. I need to tell Ellery what I'm doing. I locate her in her office despite it being nearly seven in the evening when I know she started at five this morning. These ridiculous working hours can't be good for the baby, but every time I bring up my concerns, she shoots me down.

One problem at a time. "Can we talk?"

Pain flashes in her eyes as she purses her lips and considers me. "You want to talk now?"

"Yes, if you're not too busy."

"Not too busy?" she snarks at me, and I know I messed up.

"Listen—"

"Now, you want me to listen?" Her voice raises until she's nearly shouting.

I shut the door behind me. "I'm sorry."

"Sorry for what?"

I should have known this stubborn woman won't let me get away with a mere I'm sorry.

"I'm sorry I ghosted you for the past few days. After you told me you would never leave Winter Falls, I had some thinking to do."

And I had to rearrange everything. I thought I could convince Ellery to move away from Winter Falls and follow me to Chicago. I have no idea what I was smoking that made me believe she'd move when everyone warned me about how attached to this town she is.

"You hurt me," she says in a soft whisper I don't think she intended me to hear.

I rush to her and kneel at her feet. "I'm sorry. I didn't mean to hurt you."

"It's fine." She wipes her tears away. "It's not a big deal."

"Stop," I order her. "Do not belittle your feelings. Your feelings are your feelings. If what I said or did hurt you, you need to tell me."

"I'm not… I don't know … It's not as…"

She doesn't need to finish her thought for me to understand what she's saying. She's not used to making herself vulnerable. Her college boyfriend really did a number on her and her ability to trust.

I stand and draw her to her feet. "Come on. I ordered pizza. Let's discuss this over food." Her stomach rumbles at my words and I know I've got her now.

"Fine," she gives in with a grunt.

I wait while she switches off her computer and locks her files away. Once she's finished, I grasp her hand and lead her out of the inn to the carriage house and her apartment.

"Did you tell Gracious to deliver the pizza to the carriage house or your room?" she asks as she collects plates and silverware.

"Depends." She lifts an eyebrow. "On how mad you'll be when I answer carriage house."

She sighs before asking, "What do you want to drink?"

"A beer." I need a bit of Dutch courage for the upcoming conversation. She sniffs my beer before handing it to me. "Does it bother you I'm drinking alcohol when you can't?"

She shrugs. "Not really, but I do miss beer."

"I'll pick you up some non-alcoholic beers the next time I'm at the brewery."

She rolls her eyes. "You don't have to take care of me. I can take care of myself."

She might be able to take care of herself, but I don't want her to have to. I want to be the one who takes care of her and our baby.

"Shall we sit?" I motion to the sofa, but the second my butt hits the cushions, I bounce back up again and begin pacing. I must have walked a marathon today with all the pacing I've done.

She sips on her water as she studies me from beneath her lashes. She doesn't speak, though. She waits me out. She'd probably wait me out forever. The woman is the reason the word stubborn exists.

I decide actions speak louder than words. I shove the letter into her hands. "Here."

I keep my gaze trained on her as she reads. By the time she finishes, her eyes are the size of saucers.

"Are you out of your mind?" she screeches. This is not the response I expected.

"I thought you'd be pleased."

"Pleased?" She stands and pokes my chest. "Pleased?"

I capture her hand and place it over my heart. "Yes?"

"You thought I'd be happy you quit your job? You have lost your ever loving mind!"

"No, I haven't," I defend myself. "It's just a job."

"Just a job?" She tries to wrench her hand away, but I hold on tight. "It's *the* job. The one you've wanted your entire life. The one you've been working your ass off at to make partner."

"I am aware."

"Don't be trite with me. I'm being serious here."

I cock an eyebrow. "You think I'm not being serious? I'm the one who's resigning from his job."

"I don't want you to resign. I didn't tell you about Bob and my insecurities to get you to resign."

"I know you didn't."

She carries on as if I didn't speak. "I told you because I wanted you to understand why we can't be together."

"I know." Before she can speak again, I place a finger over her mouth to stop her. "Here's the thing. We're having a baby together and I'm falling in love with you."

I didn't intend to blurt out my feelings, but she needs to know the truth.

Her mouth drops open. "Are you high?"

I chuckle. She's the only woman I know who would ask that after a declaration of love.

"I'm being serious. Did you happen to eat any food from Petal or Feather or Lennon or Basil or ..."

"I did not eat any brownies or edibles of any sort. And, before you ask, I haven't been smoking either. I'm not high, but I am falling in love with you."

She shakes her head with such force I'm afraid she'll give herself a migraine. "No. No. No. No."

I steer her to the sofa and get her settled before sitting next to her. "Ellie girl, why is it so hard for you to believe I could love you?"

"We hardly know each other."

I gather her hands in mine. "I know you're the most stubborn person I will ever meet. I know you love your family and this town with a fierceness I can't wait for you to show to our daughter."

"Son."

I ignore her interruption. She only said son to be contrary.

"I know you're the hardest working person I've ever met, which is saying a lot since I was raised by a single mom. I know you shiver whenever I touch you. And, I know you feel this connection to me, too."

She opens her mouth, but I keep talking. "I also know you're going to deny it." She pouts at my pronouncement.

"I don't want to be an absent father who sees my kid once a month and every other Christmas. I want to be there every night. Go to her ballet recitals."

"Football games."

"Those too. She can do whatever she wants," I deliberately misinterpret her words.

"What does all this mean?"

I cup her chin and meet her gaze. "It means I'm not going anywhere. It means I want to be in a relationship with you on top of co-parenting our child. A romantic relationship."

She bites her lip. I want to be the one biting her lip, but I wait to hear what her response to my announcement is. I haven't made a secret of my desire to move our relationship forward romantically, but since she told me of her past, I finally understand why she's reluctant. She's not merely being stubborn. She's scared and I don't want to spook her.

"You can't quit your job. I won't let you."

"But I don't want you to worry about my leaving. I want you to know I'm here to stay."

"And I don't want you to look back on your life and regret me and our child."

I nod. I can understand her concerns. "Which leaves us with what choice?"

She takes a deep breath and straightens her back. "You're here for two years working on the community center, aren't you?"

"Mostly," I say because I want to be completely open and honest with her. Any slight misunderstanding will break her trust. And I will have her trust. "I'll have to return to Chicago periodically but never longer than for a few days at a time."

"How about this? We see where this thing between us goes for the next two years. A few months before you're due to depart, we sit down and discuss what we both want. In the meantime, you definitely don't quit your job."

I love this idea, but it doesn't prove to her how serious I am. How I won't leave her behind and how I definitely won't cheat on her. I guess I'll have to earn her trust over the next two years.

"Okay. I agree to your conditions. And I promise I will always be honest with you. In the meantime ..."

I feather kisses along her lips until she moans. Then, I dive into her mouth. I will never get enough of her. Her taste. Her sounds. Her smell. I want it all. I gather her in my arms and set her on my lap until she's straddling me. She rocks against my cock, and I dig my hands into her hips to keep her right where she is.

Ding dong. Ding dong.

The doorbell rings and I wrench my mouth away from hers to snarl at the door. Ellie giggles.

"I guess the pizza's here."

I set her on her feet. "To be continued," I promise before stalking to the door.

Chapter Twenty-Eight

I freeze with my hand on the door to enter my parent's house for Sunday dinner. I drop my hand and step back slamming into Cole's hard body.

He squeezes my shoulders. "Don't worry."

Don't worry? Is he out of his mind? Of course, I'm worried. I've never brought a man home. My mom's not stupid. She knows I've had boyfriends before but bring them home with me? No way.

"Seriously. There's nothing to worry about. Your mom loves me. All moms do."

I whirl around to confront him. "What? How many moms have you met? Are you a serial dater?"

"Serial dater? Is that a thing?"

I wag my finger at him. "Don't be funny. I'm serious. How many moms have you met?"

"I've met a lot of moms."

I groan and bury my face in my hands. "My first boyfriend in a decade and it turns out he's a man whore."

He chuckles as he pulls my hands away from my face. "I am not a man whore. And I haven't met a ton of moms of girlfriends, but I have met a ton of women who are moms."

I slap his chest. "You were teasing me? When you know how nervous I am?"

"Thus the teasing to get your mind off your nervousness."

"You're trouble, Cole Hawkins."

He wiggles his eyebrows. "The good kind, though. Such as last night when I—"

I cover his mouth with my hands. "Shush. Do you want everyone in Winter Falls to hear about our sex life?"

"I want to hear about your sex life," Ashlyn shouts through the door.

I sigh. "Are you sure you want to live in Winter Falls?"

He shrugs. "You and the baby are here."

Not the most convincing of answers, which is the reason I won't let him quit his job. Until he falls in love with this town, he needs to keep his options open.

The door whips open. "Cole's staying in Winter Falls?"

Lilac scoffs at Ashlyn's question. "Of course, he's staying. The community center project is practically a full-time job for the next two years."

"Was everyone standing at the door listening to our conversation?"

"I was." Juniper peeks her head out the doorway and waves.

"I wasn't," Aspen shouts from the living room.

"How did you hear my question if you weren't eavesdropping?"

Before Aspen can respond, Ashlyn steps forward and nabs Cole's hand dragging him into the house. "Ellery brought her special friend to dinner."

At least, she's not referring to Cole as my baby daddy anymore.

Mom rushes out of the kitchen, her face flushed and her hair a mess. Ashlyn groans. "Don't tell me what you were doing in the kitchen. I don't want to know."

Mom grins. "Why'd you bring it up if you don't want to know?"

Dad saunters out behind Mom, slaps her ass, and winks at her before walking over to Cole to shake his hand. "Welcome to the mad house."

Mom shoves Dad out of the way before throwing her arms around Cole. "Welcome to the family."

When she releases him, he winks at me and mouths *told you so* at me. I do the mature thing. I stick my tongue out at him.

"Will you and Ellery be living in the carriage house?" Mom asks but she doesn't give him a chance to answer before plowing on. "It's okay for two people, but it's a bit small for when the baby comes. You'll need to find another place to live for the three of you. I know Saffron is considering selling her house."

I hold up my hands. "Whoa. Slow down. There's no need to discuss buying a house. Cole drew up plans to remodel the carriage house to add a nursery."

And I am not talking about whether Cole and I are living together. We decided to give being in a relationship a try a few days ago. It's way too early to discuss cohabitation. Him staying at the inn is ideal. I can see him during the day since I'm there all day anyway, and my apartment is steps away.

Although, I don't know if his company will continue to pay for a room at the bed and breakfast for the two years he's needed in town. Maybe he does need to consider finding a place to live. But purchasing a house? It's definitely too early to think about him owning a place in town.

Mom pats Cole's shoulder. "It's handy having an architect in the family."

"Hey!" Ashlyn shouts because she'll explode if she's not the center of attention. "Having a baker in the family is handy, too. Rowan brought a cake."

"Sorry, baby cakes, but I definitely win this round. Having the Chief of Police in the family is the handiest of all."

Ashlyn glares at Aspen. "What's handy about having the po-po in the family?"

Aspen crosses her arms and lifts an eyebrow. "One, he's gotten your ass out of hot water more times than I can count."

"Untrue! I have most definitely not been in trouble more times than you can count."

Rowan chuckles before pulling his wife near. He kisses her hair before mumbling, "Don't lie, troublemaker."

I scan the room. "Where is the Chief of Police?"

Aspen scowls. "Working. Someone wrote nudist on the window of Forest's pet store last night."

"Forest is a nudist," Ashlyn mumbles, but when Aspen glares at her, she holds up her hands. "Don't accuse me. I didn't vandalize his store window last night. I was with Rowan all night."

"Immediately offering an alibi doesn't exactly make you sound innocent."

Ashlyn rolls her eyes. "Don't insult me. I would never be so boring as to write nudist on a window. Someone's giving vandals a bad name."

Mom claps her hands. "Before Ashlyn climbs on her soap box to give us a lecture about vandalism, let's eat."

"I do not have a soap box," Ashlyn murmurs as she sits at the table.

Rowan and Cole sit next to each other. "What?" Cole asks when he notices me frowning at him. "There are five of you and only two of us."

My frown deepens at his comment. Is he intimidated by my family? I thought he liked them.

Dad clears his throat. "I wouldn't trade my daughters for sons for the world."

Cole smiles at me. "I hope we have a girl."

"We're having a boy."

Mom gasps and the food in her hands wobbles precariously. Dad rushes to take the tray from her before it falls to the floor. "Do you know the sex of the baby?"

"No. I don't want to know. I want it to be a surprise." I glare at Cole and wait for him to contradict me. He's been pushing me about finding out the sex of the baby since he found out I'm pregnant.

He holds his hands up in surrender. "It's your decision."

"Finally, you're getting it."

Rowan snorts. "Or you're learning how to handle a West sister."

Ashlyn pinches him. "You do not handle a West sister."

"Of course not, dream girl." He kisses her forehead.

"You have to admit it would be handy to know the sex of the baby," Aspen says, and I switch my glare to her. "What? It's easier for buying baby clothes and setting up the nursery."

"Actually, studies have shown it's better for babies to have gender neutral colors in the nursery," Lilac points out.

"Thank you, Lilac."

She studies me for a moment. "Why are you thanking me? Is this sarcasm?"

"We need to have a baby shower soon. I was thinking we could—" Mom says.

"This casserole is yummy." Aspen's shout cuts her off.

I hide my smile behind my hand. Aspen sucks at keeping secrets. She obviously started planning a baby shower but hasn't told Mom yet. Big mistake. Mom will figure it out anyway and then she'll be mad she wasn't in on the planning to start with.

"Did you use Phoenix's cheese in the casserole?" I ask before Mom can sniff out Aspen's secret. She'll sniff it out eventually – she always does – but it'll be more fun to watch the explosion when she realizes she's been left out. Someone does not like being left out.

Mom frowns. "Of course, I used Phoenix's cheese. Where else would I get cheese? Buy it from some mass producer?" Her lip curls in disgust. Sometimes, it's hard to believe she wasn't born in Winter Falls considering her advocacy for the environment and all things Winter Falls.

"Now, Cole, tell us how the community center project is going. I'm glad the town chose you to manage the project. You're obviously the most qualified. You're going to do a wonderful job."

"We didn't choose Cole. We choose his firm, *Davis Williams*." Lilac can't help herself from correcting Mom's slight error.

Cole squeezes my thigh and smiles at me. *Told you.*

I narrow my eyes on him. Is he gloating? He winks. Yep, he's definitely gloating. I return my attention to my food while he explains the progress of the project. I scan the table as he speaks and notice everyone is listening to him and nodding at his words.

Dang. He's right. There was nothing to worry about. My family has accepted him into their fold already. I rub my belly. Baby or no baby, he's a part of the West family now.

The string tethering my heart to Cole strengthens until it has the consistency of steel and with a jerk, I realize I love this man. If I'm being honest, I fell in love with him a while ago. I tried to resist but he battered at my walls with his sweet gestures and sexy ways until they crumbled.

Please don't break my heart, Cole.

Chapter Twenty-Nine

Cole

"What is Imbolic anyway?" I ask as I look around the street fair. The streets are lined with vendors selling everything from beer to organically made soap. It's crowded as tourists have invaded the town for the festival.

I grasp Ellie's hand and smile when she squeezes mine in return. Ellie and I have been a couple for nearly two weeks now. I spend most of my nights in her bed in the carriage house despite still having my room at the inn.

I don't know how long my company will pay for the room. I need to find a place to stay, but I want to stay with Ellie. She's not ready for me to move in, though. She frowns each time she notices my toothbrush next to hers on the bathroom counter.

"It's Imbolc. There's no i in it," she corrects.

"And what is Imbolc?"

"It's a celebration of the start of spring."

I snort. "The start of spring? It's freezing out here." I'm not exaggerating. We're both bundled up in winter coats, scarves, hats, and gloves.

She rolls her eyes, which are barely visible beneath her knit hat. "Don't exaggerate. You're from Chicago. You should be used to the cold."

"I didn't say I wasn't used to the cold. I said it's freezing."

"Cole! Cole!" Moon waves me over to the stand in front of the brewery. "You need to try this mulled wine. I made it myself." She thrusts a mug into my hands. "Try it. Try it."

I sip on the warm drink, and the taste of cloves and cinnamon hits my tongue. "This is good."

"Thanks. But don't drink too many." She winks.

Ellie huffs. "What did you add to the wine?"

"A splash of brandy." Moon hands Ellie a mug. "This is the kiddie punch."

"You can't say non-alcoholic?"

Moon giggles. "And miss the disgust on your face when I say kiddie punch? Nope."

I fish my wallet out of my jacket pocket. "How much?"

"It's on the house for our innkeeper and her sexy paramour."

"But—"

Ellie places a hand over my wallet. "Put it away. Your money's no good here."

I thank Moon for the drinks before capturing Ellie's hand again and resuming our journey down the street. A goat stops me when it slams into me and starts bleating up at me like I'm in his way.

"Why is there a goat in the street? Do we need to find Phoenix?"

"Don't send out a search party. I'm right here." Phoenix pats the goat on his behind and the goat wanders off toward the middle of the street where I notice an entire herd of goats.

"Why is there a herd of goats in the street?"

"It's Imbolc," he answers as if it's a perfectly reasonable response before following his goat.

Ellie giggles at my confused expression. "In addition to spring being the time of year to prepare for planting the harvest, the start of spring means the birth of lambs."

I may be a city boy, but even I know goats don't have lambs. "But these are goats and not sheep."

She shrugs. "We don't have a sheep farmer in Winter Falls, so Phoenix and his goats will have to do."

I watch as one of the goats takes a massive shit in the middle of the road. I turn away before anyone can suggest I need to clean the mess up.

"Cole!" I hear Rowan shout my name and search the area for him. I discover him standing behind a booth in front of his bakery with Ashlyn and his assistant Bryan.

Ellie hurries across the street, dragging me with her as she goes. "I can't wait to see what kind of treats he made this year."

"Hey, man," Rowan greets as we approach.

"And a mighty fine man he is," Bryan says as his eyes travel up and down my body.

"Don't pay any attention to him."

"Don't pay any attention to me! How dare you insinuate I'm not the most important person in your life?"

Ashlyn rolls her eyes. "Meet Bryan, Rowan's right hand."

"We've—"

Before I get the chance to tell her I've met him before since I've started buying Ellie treats from the bakery, Bryan speaks, "Ooooh, if I'm Rowan's right hand, does this mean I get to—"

Rowan growls at him. "There are children here."

"You don't know what I was going to say."

"Really? After working with you for over a decade, I don't know you're going to make a raunchy joke?"

"Not raunchy, funny."

"Will the two of you stop bickering now?" Ellie scowls. "The West baby is hungry."

I squeeze her hand. "I think you mean the Hawkins baby."

Rowan barks out a laugh. "Good luck with that. Your child will be known as one of those West kids no matter what her last name is."

"Her?" Bryan's eyes widen before he leans close to whisper, "Do you know it's a girl?" Ellie shakes her head. "My bet's still on a girl."

"My bet's on a boy," Ashlyn says.

I don't think they're speaking hypothetically. "Are they betting if our child will be a boy or a girl?" I ask Ellie.

She nods at me before asking her sister, "How much is the pot up to?"

Ashlyn wags her finger. "Nuh uh. No way. You can't bet on the sex of your own child. It's cheating."

Ellie snorts. "Like you're not going to bet on the sex of your child?"

"Ashlyn's pregnant!" I have to cover my ears from Bryan's high-pitched squeal.

Ashlyn frowns. "Not yet."

Ellie reaches across the table to squeeze her sister's hand. When she releases her, she announces, "I'm still hungry."

Ashlyn hands her a plate. "Try this. It's a dulce de leche buttermilk cheesecake."

"You had me at try," Ellie mumbles before stuffing half the cheesecake into her mouth at once.

She groans and suddenly I wish I hadn't forced her off the sofa and out of her apartment to come to the festival. If we were at home, I'd be the one making her groan instead of a piece of cheesecake. My pants tighten as I consider all the different ways I know to make her groan.

She glances up at me and notices the heat in my eyes. Her eyes flare in response. Oh yeah. We're getting out of here as soon as possible.

"Cole! Cole! Cole!"

I turn around to see who's chanting my name and watch as Feather, Petal, Sage, Cayenne, and Clove hurry toward us. Their faces are full of excitement, and I wish I could travel through time and lose the argument with Ellie about leaving the apartment.

"Good. You're all here," Feather says.

"We have a surprise for you." Sage smiles at me and I gulp. Knowing this group, a 'surprise' could mean anything. I do not want to know what it is, but I refuse to be afraid of five women old enough to be my grandmother.

"You're going to love it." Clove winks.

"Get out here, Rowan!" Sage shouts.

Rowan freezes with his hand on the door to the bakery where he was trying to sneak away from these women. Good grief. How bad are they to make the six-foot-five former professional football player quiver in his boots?

"I need to replenish supplies."

"I'll go," Ashlyn offers.

"You can replenish supplies in a minute after we show you our surprise." At Petal's announcement, Rowan drops his hand and trudges back to the booth.

"You ready?" The women nod at Sage's question. "Three, two, one. Tada!"

They rip open their coats and I slam my eyes shut praying it's too cold for them to be topless.

"Those are awesome," Ashlyn squeals.

Awesome? She wouldn't say their naked chests are awesome, would she? Although, it is Ashlyn. The word unpredictable was invented for her. But I won't be a chicken. I slowly open one eye until I can see Sage. She's wearing a hot pink sweatshirt with the words *Proud Gossip Gal* on it.

"I thought you preferred the term busy body?" Ellie asks.

Sage shrugs. "It's obvious certain people in this town prefer the term gossip gal." She lifts her chin toward Rowan.

"I never said gossip gal out loud."

Ashlyn snorts. "Liar."

"What happened to we're a team and we need to stick together?"

She pushes up on her toes to kiss his jaw. "You're on your own when it comes to the gossip gals."

"We are the gossip gals!" The five women begin chanting. "We are the gossip gals!"

"We have to go show the rest of Winter Falls our sweatshirts," Cayenne says.

"Don't forget to stop by *Feather's Frozen Delights*." Feather points at me. "I want your opinion on a new flavor."

"And I have a new coffee concoction for you to try, Cole," Clove adds and waves before marching off with the others.

"What am I? The guinea pig of Winter Falls?"

"They like you. They want to show you they accept you and consider you one of their own," Ellie explains.

"Congrats, man," Rowan says. "You're one of us now."

I smile at his announcement. Mere weeks ago, I would not have been happy with the idea of this community of eccentric people bringing me into their fold, but now I've accepted my future lies here – at least for the next two years – I realize how much I admire the people of this town – strange habits and all. It's not home yet, but it could be.

Chapter Thirty

"Where's the baby shower?" I ask as Cole and I leave my apartment.

He groans. "It's a surprise. You're not supposed to know."

"If you didn't want me to know, you shouldn't have laid out a dress for me to wear today."

"I told you I'm taking you out to dinner."

I indicate my watch. "It's three o'clock in the afternoon."

"At least act surprised," he mutters.

"Don't worry. I will."

I've been acting surprised and not suspicious for two weeks as the women of Winter Falls popped in at the bed and breakfast over and over again to ask my opinion about all things baby. Subtle is not a trait the residents of this town are known for.

"At least tell me it's not too far of a walk," I urge as I hobble across the parking lot. My feet are swollen, and I haven't seen my ankles in weeks.

Cole frowns when he notices my sneakers. Yes, sneakers. I agreed with the dress but there is no way I'm wearing heels. I stopped wearing pretty shoes weeks ago.

"Aspen's bookstore is too far for you to walk. I'll drive you in a golf cart." He steers me toward one of the carts parked behind the inn for guests to use at their leisure.

"We should have a code phrase," I comment as he drives us down Main Street.

He gulps as his hands tighten on the wheel. "A code phrase? I won't be staying at the baby shower. It's women only."

"It is?" I know perfectly well my shower is limited to women – the gossip gals insisted on it – but watching Cole try to control the urge to make a U-turn and return to the inn is too much fun to resist. "Co-ed baby showers are all the rage."

"I was told to drop you off shortly after three."

I burst out laughing. "Had you—" I cut myself off when the baby kicks. No, not kicks. The baby is beating a rhythm out against my belly. "This boy is going to be a drummer."

Cole pulls the cart over, and I grab his hand to place it where he can feel the baby.

"Hey baby girl," he says and the baby kicks in response. He looks up at me, the awe clear to see on his face. "She's going to be a soccer player."

"Don't say soccer in front of my dad. It's football. American football doesn't use feet."

"Whatever you call it, she's going to be the best at it." He caresses my belly. "Aren't you, baby girl?"

The baby kicks again at the sound of his voice, and I can't help but smile. "I think he likes you."

Cole leans forward to sip from my lips. "I know I'm going to love our daughter," he says when he pulls back.

"Son," I grunt, although I have to admit I'm leaning toward having a girl after observing how sweet and gentle Cole is with the baby growing inside of me.

How could I not fall in love with this man? Of course, I've yet to tell him my feelings. The idea of opening up to him scares the living daylights out of me, which is totally normal and does not make me a coward.

"You're going to be a great dad."

"I'm going to make a lot of mistakes. I didn't have the best role model."

"I'll tell Amy you said that."

I've talked to Cole's mom once a week since we met at Christmas. She wants to know everything happening with her grandchild, and I'm happy to keep her up to date.

There's a bang on the window of the bookstore. "Uh oh. The natives are getting restless. I better get in there before they start a riot in Aspen's store."

"Remember to act surprised," Cole reminds me as I walk to the door. I give him a thumbs-up before I enter the store. "Aspen? Are you here? Cole said you needed to talk to me."

The lights switch on and my older sister glares at me. "Who told you?"

I blink as I survey the room and pretend to notice the decorations for the first time. "Is this my baby shower?"

"Cut it out. We know you're not surprised. Who told?"

I shrug. "You gave it away at dinner a few weeks ago."

"Aha!" Ashlyn shouts as she bounds into the room. "I knew it wasn't me."

I snort. "Asking me a gazillion questions about what I want in my nursery wasn't exactly cunning, baby cakes."

"I was asking for my nursery," she claims.

"You keep telling yourself that."

"I certainly didn't give the secret away," Sage announces as she comes around a bookshelf with Feather, Petal, Cayenne, and Clove tagging along behind her. They're all wearing bright pink t-shirts with the words *Gossip Gal Aunt* on them.

"How many shirts do you buy?"

"We didn't buy them. We made them." The pride is clear to hear in Petal's voice. "A bit of fabric paint goes a long way."

"We're designing more styles to sell at my coffee shop," Clove adds.

I think I know what I'm getting as a gift from these ladies.

Aspen claps. "Time to get this party started." She walks to me and puts a crown on my head before handing me a sash. "For the mother to be."

"I still say the diaper crown was a better idea."

Feather gasps. "Ashlyn Dream West, you shut your mouth. We do not use disposable diapers in Winter Falls."

Ashlyn shoulders fall. "I know."

"Plus, I'm in charge, baby cakes. Not you."

Lilac rolls her eyes at Aspen's declaration. "Yes, you made it perfectly obvious you're in charge when you sent us a list of do's and don'ts for the day."

Juniper giggles. "She didn't send a list to everyone, only to you."

Lilac purses her lips but chooses not to respond.

"Here." Ashlyn presses a drink in my hands. "Don't worry. It's a mocktail."

"What? There's no alcohol in these drinks?" Moon curls her lip as she glares at her drink. "What's happened to the Ashlyn Bashlyn who's my best friend?"

"She's trying to get pregnant," I answer on her behalf.

Ashlyn growls at me. "You know darn well I didn't want the entire town knowing."

Feather pats her back. "I don't know why not. We all know a thing or two about getting pregnant."

"Doggy style is the best way to get pregnant," Petal says before asking me, "Am I right, Ellery?"

Everyone stops talking to listen to my answer. Uh oh. I know what their sudden attentiveness means. "Let me guess. There's a bet on how I got pregnant." Petal nods. "I'm not telling."

"Why don't we sit down," Aspen suggests, and I mouth *thank you* at her.

"Shall I start first?" Feather asks before opening a book and beginning to read. "Don't forget to have sex. Sex is important to—"

Aspen snatches the book from her. "You're not supposed to read your advice out loud."

"But how are we going to discuss who has the best advice if we don't read everything out loud?" Sage asks.

"I told you the book of wisdom was a bad idea," Aspen accuses Ashlyn.

"And I told you it's unnecessary," Mom says as she joins us. "Sorry, I'm late," she murmurs as she kisses my cheek. "I was busy—"

"Nope!" Ashlyn cuts her off. "No one wants to hear why you're late. It's bad enough we caught you and Dad making out in the kitchen before Sunday dinner last month."

Sage rubs her hands and leans forward. "Tell me more."

A dog whines before anyone can answer. Aspen sighs. "Juniper, I told you not to bring your dogs today."

"She's heavily pregnant. I can't leave her home alone."

"She? Bark Twain and Indiana Bones are both males." Ashlyn's eyes widen. "You got another dog?"

"Nope. I'm fostering her until her puppies are born. She already has a furever home waiting for her." Juniper winks at me. "Don't worry. I reserved one of the puppies for you."

I glance over my shoulder – surely, she isn't winking at me – but there's no one there. "I can't care for a puppy. I'm never home."

She nods to my belly. "You're going to have to slow down after the baby's born."

I am? Says who? I plan to put a crib in my office at the inn and bring the baby to work with me. No one can complain since I'm the boss.

"Juniper," Mom scolds, "you can't give a person a living animal for a present without discussing it with them beforehand."

"Are you still sore about the time I gave you a cat for your birthday? I took care of her. All you had to do was buy her cat food."

"And clean the house constantly because she shed fur everywhere."

Juniper shrugs. "Animals shed."

"I have no room for a puppy either," I interrupt before I have to listen to Mom and Juniper have the same argument for the millionth time.

Juniper waves away my concern. "Once you and Cole buy a house, I'm certain you'll have a yard for the puppy to run around in."

Buy a house? What does she know? Cole isn't in the market for a house, is he? He would tell me if he were house hunting, wouldn't he? He promised to be honest with me and omitting the truth is a lie no matter what Lilac says.

Does this mean Cole wants to live together? I love the man, but I don't know if I'm ready to live with him. Hell, I haven't gathered the courage to admit my feelings yet. Shit. I predict another discussion in my future and whenever we talk, Cole gets his way. Damn him and his logic.

Chapter Thirty-One

C^{ole}

"Hey, man!" I wave when Lyric rolls to stop next to me in front of the bookstore where I'm picking up Ellie. "Aspen drink too much at the baby shower and need a ride home?"

"Nope. She insisted on all non-alcoholic drinks."

In this town? Where they play drinking games at the monthly business meeting? I raise an eyebrow.

He chuckles. "You're catching on, but Aspen isn't drunk. I'm here to help you."

"Help me?" I look around in an attempt to figure out why I would need help from the Chief of Police, but the empty Main Street offers no clues. "Why?"

"You'll see." He motions me toward the front door of *Fall Into A Good Book.*

I follow him inside to find Ellie sitting with her feet up while she pets a dog.

"Did you make a new friend?"

She snatches her hand away. "I'm not getting a puppy," is her bizarre response.

"Um, I didn't say you were." I kneel down to the dog and scratch her ears. "If you want a puppy, I wouldn't complain. I always wanted a dog when I was growing up, but we couldn't afford one." I shrug and pretend my stomach doesn't burn at the memory.

"Yes!" Juniper shouts from behind me. "I knew you wanted a puppy for the baby."

Ellie growls at her. "I didn't say I'd take the puppy."

"But you will," Juniper sings as she leads the dog away.

"Being an only child wouldn't be such a bad thing," Ellie mutters.

I kiss her forehead before standing and holding out my hand to help her up. She groans as she gets to her feet. I bend and pick her up to carry her to the golf cart.

She slaps at my shoulders. "What are you doing? You're going to throw out your back. I'm too fat."

"You are not fat. You're carrying our precious daughter."

She huffs and crosses her arms over her chest. What she doesn't do is say anything, which means I've won this round with my stubborn girl.

I place her on the front seat of the golf cart. "I'll be right back. I'll load up your presents and afterwards, we'll go home and you can put your feet up."

I give her a brief hard kiss on the mouth before returning to the bookstore. Lyric points to a corner. "There are the presents."

I survey the stack of boxes. "This pile can't be the presents. You sure this isn't a delivery of books for the store?" The pile is huge.

Lyric bumps my shoulder as he passes me. "Told you I was here to help you."

"But where are we going to put all of this?"

I'm nearly finished building the nursery in the carriage house, but it's not the biggest nursery in the world. There's no way all of this stuff is going to fit. Ellie and I need to discuss our future living arrangements, but I know she's not ready. I sigh as I pick up the first box. Ready or not, the discussion is happening soon.

Lyric follows us to the carriage house with his load of presents.

"You can put the boxes in the carriage house for now," Ellie suggests before climbing the stairs. "I'll be in my apartment." Her apartment? The discussion of living arrangements just got moved to the top of my to-do list.

Once the presents are unloaded, I follow Ellie into her place. And it really is *her* place. I might spend my nights sleeping here with her, but she hasn't opened up to me living here at all. Every time I, accidentally on purpose, leave clothes here, they turn up in my room at the inn the next day without fail.

"Are you buying a house?" Ellie asks the second I open the door.

I guess I'm not alone in my concern about our future living arrangements. I take my time closing the door and walking to the sofa while I gather my thoughts together.

"Well, are you?"

"I don't know."

She frowns. "You don't know? How can you not know if you're buying a house or not?"

I run my hands through my hair in frustration. "Because I don't know what you want."

She rears back and her eyes fill with fear. "What do I have to do with it?"

I point at her. "This is exactly what I mean. How can you not know you have everything to do with me buying a house?"

Her nose wrinkles. "You're not making any sense."

I inhale a deep breath and remind myself Ellie hasn't been in a relationship since college. A relationship that caused her to shut herself off from men for a decade. I need to navigate this discussion with care.

I sit on the coffee table in front of her and grasp her hands. "Ellie girl, you are my future. You and our baby daughter. I want to live with you, but each time I try to bring up the subject, you shut me down."

She blinks as she stares at me. "You want to live with me?"

I squeeze her hands. "Of course, I do. I love you."

To be honest, I already loved her when I told her I was falling in love with her months ago. I knew she'd run far, far away if I told her then, though.

She gasps. "You love me?"

"It kills me that you're surprised I love you. I've tried to show you how much I care for you." I nod toward the construction of the nursery behind the living room. "But you don't see it, which makes me want to travel to Seattle and beat the shit out of Bob for how he treated you."

"I'm afraid," she whispers.

"I know you are, Ellie girl. It's why I haven't pushed us to live together."

"Do you..." she swallows, "want to live here?"

I don't think she's asking me to move in. I think she's asking what I want.

"As much as I love this carriage house. It's where our daughter was conceived after all." I waggle my eyebrows and she smiles. "I don't think it's big enough for the three of us."

"But the nursery..."

"Would make a great office for whoever lives here."

She glances around the space. "This place was a complete mess when I bought it. It was basically an empty shell. There was a raccoon family living here. Boy, were they mad when I tried to evict them." She chuckles. "I had to ask Forest to help me. He ended up sleeping in here with them until they trusted him enough to let him move them."

"Let me guess, Forest adopted the entire family, and they live with him now."

"I think he built them a house in his backyard."

I chuckle. I can't believe I initially didn't think much of Winter Falls. This town is quirky as all get out, but it's also fun and keeps me on my toes. My neighbors growing up in Chicago would keep an eye out for me, but they didn't get all up in my business and make sure I finished my homework and ate while my mom was at her second job.

"What do you say? Should we start house hunting?"

Her nose wrinkles. "But what about in two years when the community center is built?"

"We'll figure something out. I'm not going to leave you, the woman I love, or our baby daughter. I am not my father."

She cradles my face with her hands. "I didn't say you were. I know you're going to be a wonderful dad. I see it in everything you do for our baby."

I grasp her hands. "I don't do it all for our baby. I do it for you, too."

She bites her bottom lip. "You really love me?"

"I really love you," I whisper before leaning close to sip from her lips. The second our mouths meet a spark ignites between us. "Do you feel it? The connection we have?"

I wait until she nods before diving into her mouth. I need to feel her lips on mine, her tongue dueling with mine. I need to convince her she's all I see. She's all I want. I will never leave her.

She rips her mouth from mine and gulps for air. "I love you, too, Cole Hawkins." Her eyes widen, and I know she didn't mean to tell me she loves me.

I rush to reassure her. "I will treasure you for the rest of our lives, Ellery Promise."

Her mom knew what she was doing when she gave Ellery the middle name of Promise because Ellie is the promise of everything I've ever wanted in life but was too afraid to reach for.

"Maybe you should show me how much you treasure me." She throws me a saucy wink.

"I can do that." I lift her in my arms and carry her toward the bedroom. *Our* bedroom from this moment forward. Because I am not sleeping without Ellery in my arms again.

But first I plan to show her how much I love her by worshipping every inch of her body. I set her on her feet at the foot of the bed.

"Let's get this party started."

She giggles as I reach for the top button of her blouse. The sound is music to my ears. I will work my ass off to make her happy every day of my life. She deserves nothing less.

Chapter Thirty-Two

"I don't want a project," I complain to Cole as we climb the stairs to the inn after viewing yet another house. "I think I have enough of a project right now." I stroke my belly, which is now reaching epic proportions. I don't know if my skin can stretch any further if this baby continues to grow.

"But you loved the structure of the house," Cole insists.

"I loved the outside of the house. I didn't love the orange shag carpet or the green tiles in the bathroom or the linoleum in the kitchen." I huff as I collapse on the porch swing. "I don't want to time travel to the 1970s every time I walk into our home."

Our home. The idea still makes my heart seize and my feet itch to run far, far away. It wouldn't do me any good. Cole has made it perfectly obvious he'll follow me wherever I go. And I love him all the more for it.

Yes, love. It's been weeks since I told him I loved him after my baby shower, but I'm still feeling cautious. A part of me expects everything to fall apart at any minute. But whenever I notice Cole smiling at me, I can't help but want to offer him my heart on a platter.

He settles on the swing next to me and draws me near. "I guess we keep searching."

I cuddle into his side. "Too bad we can't afford the first house we viewed."

I thought having a child with someone was difficult. Ha! Agreeing to a budget for a house is the real difficulty. We argued for days. First, Cole didn't want me to contribute. I told him where he could shove his male chauvinistic ass. Then, he wanted to design and build the house. I had to remind him of the imminent arrival of our baby.

When we finally sorted out all the bullshit and agreed to a budget, we began our search. Naturally, the first house we saw was *it*. Wrap-around porch, big yard, recently renovated interior with a brand new kitchen, hardwood floors, and a master bathroom to die for. To. Die. For. The bathtub was large enough for our baby to learn to swim in it.

But the owners wouldn't come down on their asking price, which was more than fifty-thousand dollars over our budget. I was devastated. I still am. But I know better than to bring it up with Cole. He already said he's willing to go over budget for the house I love. Not happening. We have a budget for a reason.

Time to change the subject. "Have you thought about names for the baby?"

He grunts. "It's hard to come up with names when you don't know the sex of the baby."

I roll my eyes but refuse to engage in yet another argument about this. "There are plenty of gender neutral names. America, Arrow, Briar, Canyon, Cove, Freedom, Haven, Lake..."

He chuckles. "Did you buy a hippie baby naming book?"

"No." But I may have gotten one as a present at my baby shower. "Do you have a problem with hippie names?"

He shrugs. "I don't mind the names Arrow or Briar, but America and Freedom? I don't want our child to be bullied about her name."

"Cole, Cole, Cole." I tut. "Have you learned nothing about Winter Falls? The poor kid will only be bullied if he shows up at school with Jim or Stan or Tom for a name." I shiver. There will be no boring names for our child.

"I imagine the first time I lay my eyes on our baby girl, her name will come to me."

I want to correct him about the baby being a girl, but he caresses my baby bump and I get all tingly from the affection he's always showing our baby.

Whack! I sit up at the sound. "What the hell is that?"

Cole stands. "Stay here. I'll check it out."

He prowls across the porch and down the stairs. I wait until he's out of view before I follow him. I round the corner of the inn to discover him squaring off with my baby sister.

"What are you doing here?" I ask Ashlyn.

At my question, Cole whips his head around. "I told you to stay on the porch."

I roll my eyes at him before stepping forward to figure out what Ashlyn's up to now. "A shovel? Are you digging in my yard?" I'm going to kill her. "This is private property. You can't go digging around without the owner's permission."

She waves away my concern. "It's fine. I know the owner."

I growl at her. "It is not fine. I expressly forbade you from digging here."

"Which is why I planned to do this when you were away, but you came home early."

"Came home early?" What is she talking about? This is my inn. I'm here all the time.

She shrugs. "I told Saffron to keep you occupied at the house for at least an hour." She checks her watch. "But you were back within fifteen minutes."

No wonder Saffron begged us to have another look at the bathroom after I told her we wouldn't be buying the house even if the hole in the ozone layer miraculously closed.

"I thought you gave up on the Mystery of the Black Hat Bandit's Missing Loot since you're married now and trying to get pregnant."

She frowns and her shoulders hunch over. "Project Get Ashlyn Pregnant has failed yet another month."

"I'll be ..." Cole's voice trails off and he motions to anywhere but here before fast walking his ass out of here.

"It'll happen. You haven't been trying very long."

"Easy for you to say. Cole apparently has super sperm and your womb is more fertile than Phoenix's cornfield."

"Please don't tell Cole he has super sperm," I say in an effort to lighten the mood. It doesn't work.

"What if Rowan can't have children? He'll be devastated."

I pull her into my arms and hug her. A feat not easily accomplished when you're nearly eight months pregnant. "No matter what happens you two will figure it out. You fought to win the man for eight years. You'll fight to make this happen, too."

She pushes me away and wipes at her eyes. "I need a distraction from my baby failure. And my work is not a distraction. Narrating audiobooks of people having sex and getting pregnant at the drop of a hat does not help."

I flinch since I'm one of those 'got pregnant at a drop of a hat'-people. "I'll make you a deal."

"I'm not buying your baby. I know Rowan's a millionaire, but he doesn't throw his money around."

I rear back. "I'm not selling you my baby. Why would you—" I cut myself off and clear my throat. This is Ashlyn. Her mind works in mysterious ways. Ways that usually end up with her in jail.

"I meant the mystery." I indicate the shovel. "I'll allow you to dig."

She squeals and jumps for joy.

"Hold on. You haven't heard my conditions yet."

"Conditions?" She rolls her eyes. "Has Lilac commandeered your mind? If there's anyone who can figure out how to control minds, it's our robotic sister."

"As I was saying," I wait for her to nod before continuing, "you may dig in the yard, but you're limited to the area directly in front of the stone where the date 1955 is carved. You will replace the dirt when you're finished. And I will take possession of anything you discover."

"Take possession? You mean we'll review the contents together?"

"No. I mean I will keep whatever you discover for safekeeping until after this baby makes his arrival."

She frowns before holding out her hand. "I accept your conditions since it appears as if your baby's ready to pop out any minute."

I groan. "It feels like it, too, but I have at least another month to go."

"It's digging time," she shouts before sticking the shovel in the ground. She hits hard ground – it is March after all – and she grunts. "Maybe I should have brought Rowan with me."

I sigh. "I'll go get Cole."

Cole's waiting on the porch for me. "Is Ashlyn okay?"

At the concern in his voice, I fall deeper in love with him. I never imagined I could find a man who would tolerate my family let alone like them. But Cole does.

"She'll be okay, but she needs your help. She has no clue how to use a shovel. And I'm not exactly in the position to do hard labor."

He growls. "You won't be doing any hard labor on my watch."

Duh. Why does he think we need his help?

"Come on." I motion for him to follow me around the building where we find Ashlyn puffing and sweating.

"You weren't kidding when you said you needed help." Cole nabs the shovel from Ashlyn and begins digging.

"His muscles aren't as big as Rowan's but he's still pretty to look at," she remarks as we watch Cole dig.

I ignore her. I'm too busy drooling at the play of Cole's biceps as he digs mounds of dirt up. His neck strains and I can't help but think about how the muscles of his neck strain when he's doing other strenuous activities. The kind where we're both naked and sweaty while he shows me how much he cares for me.

Ashlyn waggles her eyebrows. "I'd love to know where your thoughts went."

She knows exactly where my thoughts went. Before I can tell her she will never be privy to those thoughts, Cole grunts. We rush to him.

Ashlyn drops to her knees in front of the hole he's dug. "What is it? Did you find something?"

He taps the ground and a clang rings out. "Based on the sound, I'm guessing it's metal."

"What are you waiting for? Dig it up." Ashlyn doesn't wait for him to follow her orders and starts scratching at the earth with her hands.

I grasp her hood and use my hold to draw her away. "Stop it. Rowan will kick my ass if you come home with damaged hands."

She stands and Cole uses the shovel to clear the dirt from around the metal. "It appears to be an old-fashioned lockbox."

Ashlyn bounces on her toes. "We found it. We found it. We found the loot. We're going to be rich!"

"You're already rich, remember?"

Cole digs the box out of the dirt and sets it on the lawn.

"Open it!" Ashlyn yells at him.

"No," I order. "We have a deal. I take possession of whatever you discover."

She sticks out her bottom lip. "But there could be fifty-thousand dollars in there."

"I doubt it." Cole lifts the box. "It doesn't weigh enough to be filled with cash. Plus, I can hear an object rolling around inside."

She blows out a puff of air. "It's probably another clue. Whatever. I'm out of here."

She appears dejected with her shoulders hunched over as she walks away. This is not the baby sister I know and love to annoy. Cole wraps an arm around my shoulder.

"Is she going to be okay?"

"I'll message Rowan and suggest he bring home a vat of chocolate for her. And maybe some Long Island iced teas and tequila."

He kisses my forehead. "She's lucky to have you."

"And I'm lucky to have you," I tell him.

"You sure are."

He reaches for me, but I dance out of the way. "You're filthy and you need to fix my yard."

He chuckles but returns to shoveling dirt into the hole as I pick up the lockbox and carry it inside. I'll deal with it and the mystery later when I'm not growing a baby. The baby kicks and hits my bladder. Who has time for a mystery when you need to use the restroom every fifteen minutes?

Chapter Thirty-Three

Cole

I enter our apartment to find Ellie half-asleep on the sofa. This is how I find her most days when I come home from work. She's finally slowed down. She didn't want to, but she didn't have much choice with being eight months pregnant and exhausted all the time.

I kiss her forehead. "Hey, Ellie girl. You feeling okay?"

"I'm tired, my feet hurt, and I think my skin is going to explode any second now."

"But think of the reward. In one month, you'll be holding our daughter in your arms."

"Son," she grunts, because no matter how tired the woman is she can always rally to be stubborn.

I throw my mail onto the coffee table before walking to the kitchen to begin making dinner. A task I gladly took over a few weeks ago after five nights in a row of extra-spicy Indian food. I enjoy spicy food, but unlike the pregnant Ellie, there's a limit to how much spice my digestive system can handle before it goes on strike.

"What do want to eat for dinner?"

"Chocolate ice cream and a big, fat juicy hamburger with a ton of pickles."

I chuckle. "Can we eat the hamburgers first or do we mix the two items together?"

Besides ice cream and spicy food, Ellery hasn't had many pregnancy cravings. There have been no middle of the night trips to the convenience store, which is a good thing since Winter Falls doesn't have a convenience store and *Nature Coop* closes at eight every night without fail.

"Ice cream first."

I grab a carton of chocolate ice cream from the freezer – which I quickly learned to keep stocked with chocolate ice cream and frozen chocolate chip cookie dough – and hand the carton to Ellie along with a spoon. She cuddles it to her chest before diving in.

When she moans, I growl. "You're killing me, Ellie girl."

Her gaze meets mine, and I notice chocolate ice cream smeared around her face. Pregnant Ellery is not a clean eater. I want to lick the ice cream from her face before exploring more inventive places to lick ice cream from her body.

Her eyes flare but she blinks, and the heat dies before she wags her spoon at me. "Food now. Sex later. Little Freedom's hungry."

I roll my eyes at her reference to the baby as Little Freedom. She knows I don't want our daughter to be named Freedom, which means she uses every opportunity she can to call the baby by that name.

"Do you still want a burger?"

She gasps and drops the spoon in the ice cream. "Cole Hawkins, you're not depriving the mother of your child of dinner, are you?"

"I wouldn't dare," I mutter before leaning down to kiss her forehead. "I'll start the grill."

I'm at the door when she gasps. "What's this?"

Shit. She found the letter. I considered throwing it away, but I didn't want her to find out about the letter some other way, and trust me, she would. I don't know how, but it's impossible to keep a secret in this town. I wouldn't be surprised if the gossip gals take turns searching everyone's trash.

"It doesn't matter."

"Doesn't matter? Now I have to know what it is."

"Curiosity killed the cat."

"Good thing I'm not a cat." She snatches the letter out of the envelope. She doesn't read long before her eyes widen, and she gasps again. "How does this not matter?" She fists the letter and shakes it at me.

I sigh before sitting in front of her and snatching the letter from her. "Because I'm not interested in another job."

I was shocked when I received the letter today. As I haven't been searching for another job, a letter from a headhunter came as a complete surprise. When I discovered I'd been scouted for a job with one of the biggest architectural firms in the country, I wanted to run to Ellery to share my news.

But she wouldn't understand. I knew she'd confuse my feeling flattered with excitement about the job. I'm not excited about the job. I don't want another job. I'm perfectly content with my current job.

"*Albrecht and Bettencourt* is considered the premier architectural firm in sustainable building," she recites from their website. "The firm has projects throughout North America. These projects include—"

I snatch the phone out of her hands. "I know who *Albrecht and Bettencourt* is."

She pushes to her feet. "Then, you know you need to accept this job."

"It's not a job offer. It's a request to interview."

She waves away my response. "Same difference."

"No, it's not..." I cut myself off. It doesn't matter. "Why are we arguing about this? I'm not interested in another job for the foreseeable future." My eyes dip to her swollen belly.

"Oh no, you don't! You are not going to ruin your career for me and this baby!" she screams at the top of her lungs.

I hold my hands up in a soothing gesture. "Calm down, Ellie girl."

She bats my hands away. "Calm down? Don't you know better than to tell a woman to calm down?"

I risk her wrath and shackle her wrists. "Ellie girl, you have to think of the baby. An elevated heart rate isn't good for her."

She stares daggers at me, but she does inhale deep breaths in and out until the red hue on her face fades. She yanks her hands away. "I'm calm."

"Good." I kiss the tip of her nose. "I'll get the grill started for those burgers."

"Stop!"

Crap. So much for diverting her attention with the promise of food. To be honest, it wasn't my best plan.

"Can we discuss this letter?"

Her voice is deceptively soft. I know better. I'm not having this discussion with her. She almost didn't give me a chance because I'm not from Winter Falls. A job in New York City will be the perfect excuse for her to end things with me. Not happening.

"There's nothing to discuss. I'm not in the market for a new job. I have the community center project, remember?"

"Stop being dismissive. This is a huge opportunity for you. It's better than making partner at *Davis Williams*."

Damn it. I had to fall in love with a woman who actually listens to everything I say and remembers it. I made some offhand comment about *Albrecht and Bettencourt* being the ideal firm I couldn't imagine working at in my dreams months ago. She shouldn't remember.

"Whether or not it's a huge opportunity is immaterial. Listen to what I'm saying. I. Am. Not. Interested."

"Would you have been interested if it weren't for me and the baby?"

Fucking hell. How do I answer this question without hurting her? Without damaging our relationship? I promised her honesty and honesty is what she's getting. I hope I'm left standing when she hears what I have to say.

"To be honest, yes." Her face falls and I palm her neck to bring her close until our foreheads touch. "But things change. I've changed. I fell in love with this stubborn as all get out innkeeper and she's having our baby. I'm not leaving Winter Falls, even if it is for my dream job."

Her eyes well and I realize I've gone too far. I should have left the last bit out. There is such a thing as too much honesty. I'm a fucking idiot.

"It's not the dream job," I backpedal.

"It is *your* dream job," she whispers as the dam breaks and tears tumble down her cheeks.

"And you're my dream woman. The woman I didn't realize I was searching for. I love you, Ellery Promise West." I kiss her eyelids and taste the salt of her tears. "I can't wait to meet our daughter."

She pushes me away. "I can't let you do this." She sniffs and I reach for her, but she backs away. "I can't let you ruin your life for me. You'll resent me. I can't have the man I love resenting me."

A fist squeezes my heart. "What are you saying?"

"I'm saying you need to go. You need to accept this job."

"It's not a job offer," I push out through gritted teeth.

"You've been headhunted for this job. It's as good as."

"I am not interviewing for a job I don't want to make you feel better."

"Oh yes, you are. Leave!" She points to the door. "Go! Go to your stupid interview for your stupid job and leave me alone."

I open my mouth to argue with her, but if there's one thing I've learned about Ellery Promise West, it's that when her mind is set, you need to give her time to calm down. I'll give her time, but I won't be going to any interview.

"This is not goodbye or the end," I declare. "If I leave here now, it changes nothing between us."

"It changes everything," she whispers before retreating to our bedroom to hide.

I slam the door and stomp down the stairs. She kicked me out. She fucking kicked me out. I know it's because she's stubborn and scared, but it still stings like a bitch.

There's only one thing I can do. I need to come up with a way to prove to her once and for all, I'm not leaving. I'm never leaving. No matter what company comes calling, I'm in Winter Falls to stay.

Chapter Thirty-Four

I don't bother greeting Aspen when she answers the phone. I blurt out, "He's gone."

"Who's gone? What are you talking about?"

"Cole. He left."

After I cried myself to sleep last night, I woke up alone in bed with puffy eyes and a shattered heart. I know I told Cole to leave, but I didn't think he would. I thought he'd sleep at the inn for the night and be back this morning to fix me breakfast.

When he wasn't at home, I ventured to the inn to search for him. I couldn't find him anywhere. None of the unoccupied rooms have been slept in. And Soleil didn't check anyone in before she got off shift last night.

Once I realized he wasn't at the inn, I ran to the parking lot to check for his Jeep. It's gone. Which means, Cole's gone. Well and truly gone.

"I'm on my way," Aspen says and hangs up.

I throw my phone toward the coffee table where it bounces a few times before skidding off. I don't bother picking it up. No one's calling who I want to hear from anyway. The inn will have to survive a day without me. I'm in no state to handle guests or their toilet paper emergencies.

Literally, I'm in no state. I haven't washed my face let alone combed my hair or brushed my teeth. Why bother?

"Oh boy," Aspen says when she enters. "Someone's having a pity party."

"Where?" Ashlyn asks as she pushes past her. "I don't see a pity party. There's no chocolate, no tequila, no Long Island iced teas."

"A pregnant woman shouldn't be drinking Long Island iced teas or tequila," Lilac says as she walks in.

Ashlyn rolls her eyes. "I know. I read your emails. What I don't know is how to comfort a broken-hearted woman without alcohol. There should be a rule book for comforting teetotaling women."

"I know how to comfort her," Juniper shouts from behind the group. The group parts and Juniper marches in carrying a fluffy puppy. "Don't worry. I know you can't handle a puppy right now. I'll keep her until she's potty trained, but a cuddle from this fluffy ball of fur is exactly what the doctor ordered."

She dumps the blonde furball into my lap and the puppy immediately pushes up on her hind legs to lick my face. She's not very steady on her feet, though, and she falls to the side and ends up licking my arm.

I lift her up until I'm eye to eye with her honey-colored puppy eyes. "She's adorable. What's her name?"

"She's your puppy. You get to name her."

"Honey. I'm going to name her Honey." The pup yips and licks my cheek. "She already knows her name. You're the smartest dog in the world."

Juniper dusts her hands off. "My work here is done." She bows. "Goodbye and goodnight."

Ashlyn grabs her before she can walk out the door. "You're not seriously leaving, are you?"

Juniper rolls her eyes. "It was a joke. Of course, I'm not leaving. I do win sister of the month, though."

Ashlyn holds up a bag with the logo from *Bake Me Happy* on it. "Not all the votes are in yet."

"What did you bring?" I ask, the puppy momentarily forgotten.

"I told Rowan to give me one of everything with chocolate."

"What are the rest of you going to eat?"

Lilac purses her lips. "I don't think an overabundance of chocolate is good for the baby. Chocolate contains caffeine."

"And I don't think I care right now. When the man you love walks out on you, you're allowed to eat all the chocolate you can regardless of your state of pregnancy."

"Walks out on you?" Aspen asks before flopping down on the sofa next to me. "What happened?"

I ponder how to answer her question while my sisters gather around me. Juniper steals the puppy from me and lays on the floor with her.

"It's my fault," I say because it is. "I should've never believed an out-of-towner would want to stay in Winter Falls."

"What about the community center? Is another architect from *Davis Williams* being sent to oversee the project?"

"I don't give the first shit about the community center," I snarl at Lilac.

"It was a perfectly reasonable question."

Ashlyn rolls her eyes. "Yeah, if you don't feel emotions."

"I feel emotions. Why does everyone think I don't have emotions? I'm human. All humans feel emotions. Granted people express their emotions in different ways, but everyone has them."

I hold up my hand before Lilac begins a lecture on human emotions. Knowing her, she has one prepared. My sister may have robotic tendencies, but she's wicked smart and retains every bit of information she encounters.

Aspen clears her throat. "We'll circle around to the community center and human emotions."

"Oh please, no," Juniper mumbles but Aspen ignores her.

"What I want to know is why Ellery thinks it's her fault Cole left."

Ashlyn raises her hand. "Me too."

"He got a job offer from another architecture firm."

"*Albrecht & Bettencourt*?" Lilac asks.

I narrow my eyes at her. "How do you know?"

"A recruiter called and asked for a recommendation for Cole."

My eyes narrow, and I spit laser beams at her. "What the hell, Lilac? You didn't think to tell me?"

She shrugs. "Why would I tell you? He's committed to you. You're having a baby together. He's not going to accept a job in New York City."

"Wrong! Where do you think he is at this very moment?"

She checks her watch. "He can't be in New York City. He'd never have made it there by now."

"Someone strangle her for me. I'm too pregnant to roll off this couch and do it myself."

Ashlyn springs to her feet. "I got your back." She cracks her knuckles as she stalks toward Lilac.

Lilac doesn't appear intimidated. "What are you doing?"

Ashlyn tilts her head back and cackles. "I'm going to suck your blood."

Lilac sighs. "You do know vampires don't exist?"

I pick up a pillow and throw it at her. "Lilac Bean West, stop being so damn literal."

Her cheeks pinken. "Sorry."

"Does this mean I don't get to slap her around a bit?" Ashlyn mimes slapping someone in the face.

Juniper dumps the puppy in my lap. "I think you need more cuddle time."

I cradle the puppy to me like she's a baby. "What am I going to do with you, Honey? I won't have a yard now. Do you want to live in an apartment?"

At least Cole finished the nursery before he left. It'll be a tight fight with me and the baby and now a puppy in the carriage house, but I can make it work.

"The parking lot literally backs up to the forest. I think you have enough space to walk Honey," Juniper points out.

"Is there any chance we can hear what happened between Cole and Ellery before I decide to commit fratricide?" Aspen grumbles.

"I think you mean sororicide. Fratricide refers to killing a brother. Sororicide refers to killing a sister," Lilac explains.

"Nope, no chance," Ashlyn mumbles around the muffin she has stuffed in her face.

"Hey! You're eating my chocolate."

She throws me a cookie. "There's plenty for everyone."

"Will everyone stop enabling Ellery and her desire to avoid telling us what happened?"

I stick my tongue out at Aspen. She couldn't let me continue to avoid the topic?

"Get it over quick. Like pulling a bandage off," Juniper suggests. "Afterwards, we can move on to chocolate and chick-lit movies."

"Cole said he'd be interested in the job if it weren't for me and the baby, so I told him to go to the interview."

"Wait! Hold up!" Ashlyn shouts. "You told Cole to leave? You kicked him out?"

"I didn't think he'd go anywhere. I thought he'd show up this morning to talk everything through. He loves to talk things to death. Instead, he proved to me what I've known from the start. He's not serious about staying in Winter Falls," I say and promptly burst into tears.

Honey yips and scratches to escape my hold. Juniper rescues the puppy before Aspen throws her arm over my shoulder and hugs me close. "Oh, Ellery, I'm sorry."

Lilac presses a tissue in my hand. "I, too, am sorry. It appears I misjudged Cole."

"You didn't misjudge Cole," Ashlyn announces. "He'll be back."

"No, he won't," I blubber. "His car is gone. This is Winter Falls, if he were in town, I'd know it."

Since they can't deny the truth of what I'm saying, no one replies.

"I should have never gotten involved with a man. I know better. I don't need a man."

Juniper throws her hands in the air. "You preach it, sister."

Aspen pats my back. "Not all men are bad. I promise you. Someday you'll find the man for you."

"In the meantime, you have another little man to think of." Juniper nods to my belly.

"I want a little girl," I howl.

I can't have a boy. He'll resemble Cole and every time I look at him, I'll be reminded of what an idiot I am. No, a girl is the safer choice. A girl the entire town of Winter Falls will help me raise. She won't need a father. Furthermore, she won't miss him. I'll make damn sure of it.

Chapter Thirty-Five

Cole

"You certain you want to do this?" Lyric asks as he helps me carry the sofa into the house.

"It's a bit late for second guessing, don't you think?"

We set the sofa down and I sweep my hand out to indicate the living room of the house I bought yesterday.

"You can always co-parent with Ellery. You don't need to buy her a house and marry her," Rowan says as he comes up behind me.

I growl at the two. "What the hell is this? I love Ellie. She's having my daughter and we're getting married. End of discussion."

Rowan slaps me on the back, and I have to plant my legs to stop from pitching forward at the force. "Just checking."

"Yeah." Lyric's pat on my arm has the power of a punch, but I grit my teeth and hide my reaction. "The way you ran out of town the minute things with Ellery got tough, we needed to make sure."

"I didn't run out of town, and you damn well know it."

I did leave the inn, but only because I needed to concoct a plan to prove to Ellie how serious I am about staying in Winter Falls. To show her I'm not going to run away at the first job offer thrown my way.

I soon realized I didn't have anywhere to go, though. I couldn't stay with Lyric without Aspen knowing. Same for Rowan and Ashlyn finding out. I didn't want her sisters to know I didn't flee town before Ellery knows. Which left me with one option. My soon-to-be in-laws.

"Don't mind me," Mrs. West says as she flutters through the living room toward the stairs. "I'm not listening."

Her husband grunts as he follows her into the house. "Don't believe her. She's always listening."

"Mr. West." I nod at the man. "Can I have a word?"

"I hope your word is asking for my daughter's hand in marriage. Unlike these two ungrateful jackasses, a father prefers to be asked."

"Liar," Mrs. West shouts from upstairs.

"I told you. She's always listening."

"I'm not ungrateful," Rowan begins. "But if you've met your daughter, you know there was no force on this earth strong enough to keep me from marrying Ashlyn once she decided on a Vegas wedding."

"You're going to have to learn to control her or she's going to run roughshod all over you during your marriage."

"Daniel West. No one controls our daughters."

"She could at least pretend she's not eavesdropping," he mumbles.

"And I did ask for your daughter's hand in marriage," Lyric claims.

Mr. West frowns. "You were sixteen at the time, and I said no."

Lyric shrugs. "But I asked."

"Can I have a word in private?" I ask again.

"There's no need for privacy. You can ask for Ellery's hand now."

"Do you have a ring?" Mrs. West shouts down the stairway.

"Yes."

"I approve."

"He's not asking you, Ruby. He's asking me. Man to man."

"Then, be a man and give him your approval. I need your help putting this changing table together."

"Mr. West," I begin.

"You might as well call me Daniel. We'll be family soon whether or not you convince my daughter to forgive you and marry you."

Fuck. Is there a chance she won't forgive me? She has to forgive me. My life begins and ends with her.

"You don't think she'll forgive me? I bought her the house she wanted to show her I'm not leaving her."

He slaps me on the back. "That's all I needed to hear. Now, I need to go help my better half."

"Beer?" Lyric asks as he grabs three bottles from the refrigerator.

I hold up my hand and he tosses it to me before tossing the other one to Rowan who holds up his bottle. "Welcome to the family."

"Knock knock." Sage doesn't wait for a response before charging into the house with Feather, Petal, Cayenne, and Clove hot on her heels.

I wipe a hand down my face. "You're not supposed to know I'm here."

Feather snorts. "Young man, if we weren't helping to hide you in Winter Falls, Ellery would already be here giving you a piece of her mind."

I glance at Lyric, and he nods. "It's true. These ladies are the only reason the West sisters haven't found out what you're up to yet."

"And stormed in here to demand retribution," Rowan adds.

Retribution?

"We'll start in the kitchen," Sage announces before removing her coat to reveal a hot pink t-shirt with the words *Gossip Gal Welcome Wagon Member* on them.

"What have I done?" Rowan mumbles beside me.

"Um." I search for the proper response. "Thank you for your offer of help, but we're nearly finished."

Feather bursts out laughing. "Nearly finished?" She pats my arm as she passes me.

"We are nearly finished," I insist.

"Men." Cayenne huffs. "They have no clue a house isn't a home unless it's decorated."

"I'm an architect. I'm perfectly aware of the difference between a house and a home."

I might not have spoken for all the effect it has. Cayenne talks over me. "Decorations are important. Where are the pictures? The knick-knacks? There's not a single pillow on the sofa."

"I want Ellery to put her stamp on the house. She can put up the pictures and decorate with throw pillows and whatnot."

"Ah, isn't he cute?" Petal reaches forward to pinch my cheeks. I don't think anyone's pinched my cheeks in thirty years.

"We'll go on one condition," Sage offers, and I can feel Rowan and Lyric inching away from me. Chickens.

"What condition?"

"I expect to babysit the baby when he arrives."

"She," I say automatically.

"Oh, a daughter," she squeals. "It's been too long since I cared for a little girl." She leans close to whisper, "Between you and me, Ruby was awful selfish with her daughters. She never let me babysit them."

"I did, too," Ruby claims as she and Daniel bound down the stairs to join us. "But there was no way I was going to allow you to watch them again after you let them eat a gallon of ice cream."

Sage shrugs. "I didn't realize Aspen was tall enough to reach the freezer."

"You should have been watching them and noticed before they managed to eat most of the ice cream." Ruby turns to me. "The ice cream ended up on the floor, in their hair, on their clothes, on the walls, everywhere. Ashlyn was a baby, so you can imagine where her ice cream ended up."

"I can't help it if Feather phoned with news while I was babysitting the girls."

Feather wags a finger at Sage. "Don't you dare blame me for your babysitting mishaps."

"Ever and Radiance never complained when I babysat Lyric, River, and Phoenix."

Ruby crosses her arms over her chest. "Maybe because they didn't have a phone installed in the farmhouse meaning you couldn't get distracted by gossiping with your cronies."

"I prefer the word busybody," Clove announces.

"Me, too." Feather nods. "But gossip gal has a nice ring to it. Did you notice our shirts?"

"The astronauts on the International Space Station noticed their shirts," Lyric mumbles behind me.

"We didn't realize hot pink meant bright pink," Cayenne explains. "And by the time we did, the boxes had been delivered."

"But the bright pink does match well with the silver sparkly fabric paint," Petal says.

The women begin debating the merits of the various types of fabric paint and I decide now is a perfect time to escape. I'm not alone. When I step out on the back porch, Daniel, Rowan, and Lyric are already there. I lift my beer to them in a salute.

Daniel frowns. "You couldn't have snagged me a beer on your way?"

I peer through the window and try to calculate the distance between the women and the refrigerator. Maybe I can make it without them noticing me?

Rowan pushes past me. "You need a professional for this."

"Former professional," Lyric quips, and Rowan flips him off before opening the door and rushing to the refrigerator.

He has the beer in his hand and is opening the sliding door to the backyard before the women notice him. He holds up the beer and opens the door with his other hand. "I need to deliver this to Mr. West."

"At least you know you have the gossip gals' seal of approval," Rowan comments after he shuts the door behind him.

I cock my brow. "I do?"

"You think they'd be here busting your chops if you didn't have their approval?" he asks.

Lyric motions to them with his beer. "This is how they show their love."

Daniel lifts his beer. "Welcome to Winter Falls."

I clink his beer, but I don't take a sip. I'm too busy wondering how soon I can have a security system installed to keep the busybodies of Winter Falls out of my house. And here I thought winning my Ellie back was the biggest obstacle in my future.

Chapter Thirty-Six

"I don't want to go," I pout.

Aspen shackles my wrist before dragging me down the street. "Too bad. You're going."

"Yeah, stinky." Juniper wrinkles her nose. "You needed to shower and get out of the house."

"Huh." Ashlyn grunts. "I didn't realize you can actually smell considering you live with Bark Twain aka the farty dog."

"He can't help it he has digestive issues."

"Yeah, right. His 'digestive' issues have nothing to do with his propensity for eating anything he finds laying around on the floor."

"I am sometimes confused how I'm related to the rest of you," Lilac comments.

"Back at ya, sister," I mutter.

I try freeing my wrist, but Aspen doesn't let up on her hold. "Sorry, sis, but I can't trust you to not run back home."

"What's wrong with home? I'm a million months pregnant, my feet are swollen to the size of clown shoes, and I need to pee. Again."

Lilac studies my feet. "Clown shoes are sixteen inches long. Your feet aren't anywhere near the correct size."

I stop to stare at her. "How the hell do you know what size clown shoes are? I'm serious. I get you're a brainiac when it comes to all things science but clown shoes? They have nothing to do with science."

Her cheeks darken. "My boss asked me to arrange a birthday party for his sister. There were clowns involved. Please, don't make me repeat the story."

"You are definitely repeating the story," Ashlyn declares.

"But not now." Aspen taps her watch.

"Are we on a time schedule?"

She glances away. "No."

"You're a sucky liar."

"Am not."

"Are too."

Lilac claps her hands. "While I'm enjoying this debate immensely, we are on a time schedule."

"You aren't supposed to tell her we're on a time schedule," Aspen growls.

Lilac shrugs. "You didn't inform me I'd be lying today."

"Hold up!" Ashlyn shouts. "I don't care about the lying. I care about Lilac using sarcasm. Did everyone hear it?"

Juniper's hand shoots into the air. "I did."

Ashlyn hugs Lilac. "I'm so proud of you."

Lilac stands there, stiff as a board, patting Ashlyn's back. I'd be amused if I weren't worried about what the heck my sisters are up to. And they're definitely up to something.

"Come on." Aspen motions us forward. "We can make Lilac a certificate commemorating her first use of sarcasm later. First, we need to get to—"

I wag my finger at her. "Oh no, you don't. Tell me where we're going this instant or I'm going home."

Aspen giggles as she threads her arm through mine. "I admire how you think you can take the four of us on while you're pregnant. Delusional but admirable all the same."

"Where's my phone?" I mutter. "I need to call the police."

"Don't worry. Lyric's waiting for us."

My brow wrinkles. "Lyric? Why is your fiancé waiting for us?" My eyes widen. "Is this a surprise wedding?" I glance down at my outfit. "Is this why you made me wear a dress?" The dress is reminiscent of a muumuu but at least I'm not wearing the stained sweatpants and t-shirt I had on when they invaded my home thirty minutes ago.

"I am not having a surprise wedding, unlike some people."

Ashlyn shrugs. "I wasn't surprised. I knew why we were flying to Vegas the whole time."

"You need to plan your wedding party before Mom loses her mind," I remind her.

"I'm safe. I should probably thank you for getting pregnant when you did. Mom's too excited with the idea of her first grandchild coming into the world to be very angry at me for eloping."

I rub my hand over my belly. Too bad the baby's dad isn't excited about the idea of having his first child and upped and left town without so much as a goodbye. He said his leaving wasn't a goodbye but what else am I supposed to believe?

I haven't heard a peep from him in a week. Not one message asking how I'm doing or how the baby's doing. He probably already found a new woman in New York City. A fancy woman to match his fancy new job.

We slow as we reach my dream home Cole and I viewed. I can't help but imagine myself lazing on the front swing while the baby crawls on the porch and the puppy runs around the yard. I notice the lawn's been mowed and the rose bushes have been trimmed.

"I guess someone bought my house."

I wasn't holding my breath hoping I could somehow figure out how to afford this place, but my heart still squeezes when I realize this place will never be my home.

"Let's keep going to wherever it is we're going."

When no one responds to my statement, I glance over my shoulder and realize my sisters are slinking away. What the hell?

"What are you doing?" I shout my question to Aspen who's dashing around the corner of the house to the backyard. She gives me a thumbs-up but doesn't stop.

Someone clears his throat and I whirl around to find Cole standing before me. My hands fist on my hips. "What are you doing here? Shouldn't you be in New York?"

"I'm right where I want to be."

He takes my hand and draws me forward. I plant my feet. I'm not going anywhere with the man who runs out on me at the first hurdle.

"You can walk on your own two feet or I'm carrying you."

"Carrying me? Have you missed how large I am?" I indicate my belly.

He smiles. "No, I have not." He kneels in front of me to cradle my stomach. "Hey, baby girl. Have you missed me?" The baby kicks in response to his voice. "I've missed you too, baby girl." He kisses my belly before standing and holding out his hand to me.

I stare at it for a long second before reaching forward. I'm probably being a fool, but I can't seem to resist this man. He clamps down on my hand as if he doesn't ever want to let me go. *Stop those fanciful thoughts, Ellery. You know better.*

We walk up the steps to the porch, and he opens the front door. I yank on his hand. "I told you. We can't afford this house," I hiss. "I don't want to view it again. Besides, I think someone already bought it."

"Someone did," he says as he tugs me inside. "Welcome home, Ellie girl and baby girl."

"Little Freedom," I grunt to annoy him, but then I scan the interior and forget all about annoying him.

The house doesn't resemble the place we viewed a few weeks ago. It's no longer an empty shell with all the furniture filling it. The living room has a corner sofa, in front of which is an entertainment center with an obnoxious sized television. In the dining room, there's an oversized farm table. Making things even weirder, it's currently covered with an array of food.

Cole wraps his arms around me from behind and props his chin on my shoulder. "What do you think of your new home?"

New home? What's he talking about? "It's gorgeous, but—"

"Do you want to see the upstairs before you decide?" He steps away and grasps my hand. "The nursery's all set as is the master bedroom. Of course, you'll need to bring life to the place. Put your own stamp on it."

I tug on his hand before he can drag me upstairs. "What's going on, Cole? You left last week to interview for a job in New York City and now you've bought a house?"

He cups my cheeks. "I never left Winter Falls."

"Impossible. I would have known if you were in town."

"I had help." He nods toward the patio doors where the gossip gals are plastered to the glass trying to eavesdrop.

"But you went silent. No messages. No calls. Nothing."

"You didn't reach out to me either."

I frown. It's true. I didn't. "I thought you were done with me."

He kisses my nose. "I'll never be done with you, Ellie girl. I want to spend my life with you and our baby girl."

"Little Freedom."

He rolls his eyes before continuing. "After your reaction to the letter, I knew I needed to do something to convince you I wasn't leaving. It didn't take me long to figure out what. Unfortunately, I did need some time to get the mortgage approved and the sale processed."

"You bought this house for me?"

"No," he says, and I wonder if I got it all wrong. "I bought this house for us. For our family." He leans his forehead against mine and whispers, "I love you, Ellery Promise West."

For the first time, I believe him. Really believe him. He's not letting me go. He will fight to keep our family together.

"I love you, too." He sips from my lips, but I draw back. I've got more to say. "I'm sorry I acted like a bitch about the letter. All my old insecurities reared their ugly heads and I lost it."

"It's my fault. I should have handled the situation with more care. I knew you'd consider the letter a threat, but I wasn't prepared."

"It's over now." It's true. It's over. I won't let my insecurities ruin my life with Cole.

"You believe I'll stay? I won't run away?"

I roll my eyes. "You bought us a house – *the* house – in my hometown. Of course, I believe you'll stay. I also promise to not push you away in the future."

"Good." He kisses my nose before dropping to his knee.

My eyes widen. "What are you doing?"

Bang! Bang! Bang! Sage slaps her hand against the glass door. "Cole Hawkins! You promised to ask her outside in front of the town."

"How big of trouble am I in if I ask you now instead of outside?"

"Ask me what?" I wink.

He opens his palm to show me a diamond ring. "Be my forever?"

I tap my chin and pretend to contemplate the question.

"Go on. Say yes. You know you want to."

"Fine," I pretend to huff. "I guess I'll marry you. Since I'm having your baby and all."

"Nope. I'm not marrying you because you're carrying my child. I'm marrying you because I want to wake up next to you every morning for the rest of my life, although I do plan to work on getting you to stop helping with the breakfast service since a five a.m. wake-up call is ridiculous."

I am not discussing my workaholic tendencies with him while he's on his knee proposing. Especially since he's kind of right. I won't be admitting I'm wrong any time soon, though.

I wave my hand at him. "Put the ring on me. I want to go show it off."

He slides the ring on my finger, and I admire it as the diamond sparkles. He pushes to his feet and grabs my hand before leading me up the stairs.

"I thought we were going outside to show everyone my ring."

He smirks. "I need to show you something in the bedroom first."

I tug on his hand until he stops in the upstairs' hallway. "I love you, Cole Hawkins. I can't wait to be your wife."

"Thank you, Ellie. Thank you for giving me a family."

I don't have a chance to tell him he's welcome before his lips are on mine and I forget what I was going to say.

Chapter Thirty-Seven

Juniper

I scan the backyard filled with my family and friends. It's the perfect day to celebrate an engagement. My phone buzzes in my pocket. Not completely perfect after all. Why can't he leave me alone?

You'd think he'd have gotten the hint by now. We're over. Although, we never really actually began. It's hard to have a relationship when half of the couple rushes off the morning after sex. Once, I'd understand. I may have even understood twice. But when he hit double digits, I was done.

"Here." Aspen presses a glass into my hand.

I sniff the drink and nearly rear back at the strong scent of alcohol. "What is this?"

"A martini."

"This is not a martini."

"Yes, it is. Gin and vodka equals martini."

I shiver. "What about the vermouth?"

"Trust me. You're going to need the fortification."

I pause with my lips on the glass. "What are you talking about?"

"It's your turn."

"My turn?"

Lilac and Ashlyn join us.

"I believe she means she's going to meddle in your love life next," Lilac says.

I retreat a step. "What about you? Why can't she meddle in your love life?"

"Please," Aspen draws out the word. "I think we all know Lilac will be the last of us to pair off, and she's going to need the most help. It's for the best if all of us are happily paired up before we set our sights on matching Lilac."

"What if I don't want to be happily paired off?"

Ashlyn barks out a laugh. "Liar."

"I am not lying," I sneer at her.

I'm done with men. Men who make tons of promises before they get you in their bed and then disappear before you wake up the next morning. Men who can't be bothered to answer your calls until you start ignoring them. I hate games. In fact, I'm thinking I hate most people at the moment.

The crowd buzzes and I glance over at the back porch expecting to see Ellery and Cole emerge from the house. It's about time. But the happy couple is still missing from their own party.

"Someone's not a secret admirer anymore," Ashlyn sings.

I scan the crowd and there he is. Maverick Langston. Shit.

Aspen and Lilac stare at him with their mouths hanging open as he stalks across the lawn toward us.

"You knew about him?" Aspen asks Ashlyn before he reaches us.

"Of course. Juniper and I don't have secrets."

I snort. "She means she followed me to work and spied on me."

"Same thing."

"June bug," Mav greets in his deep voice, and I nearly forget why I've been ignoring the man. He smirks and I remember. He's a movie star who's playing at being with me. He's not really interested in me as a person. Hell, he's not interested in the wildlife refuge except as a tax write-off.

I tag his hand and pull him toward the edge of the yard. "What are you doing here?" I hiss at him. "You've blown your cover."

"No, he hasn't," Sage says before Maverick can respond. "We've known Rickie owned the Wildlife Refuge since he bought it."

"Nothing is sacred in this town," I grumble.

"Sacred refers to—"

I shove my palm in Lilac's direction. I don't need a lecture on the proper use of the word sacred right now.

"Can't you give us some space to have a private conversation?" I ask when I notice everyone followed us.

"Why would we do that?" Aspen asks.

"I've never met a movie star before. I want an autograph," Ashlyn adds.

I roll my eyes at her. "You're a big fat liar. Half of your college graduating class became movie stars."

"I wouldn't say stars," she mumbles.

"Who is this man?" Lilac asks.

"It's Maverick Langston. If you'd been to any of Juniper's monthly movie nights, you'd recognize him," Ashlyn explains.

"Enough!" I shout loud enough for the entire town to hear me. "Everyone needs to back off before the revealing of secrets begins."

"I don't have any secrets," Sage shouts.

I cock an eyebrow. "How about the time I saw you—"

"Let's give Juniper and Rickie some space," she says before I can finish tattling on her. She herds everyone toward the house.

"Now," I turn my attention to Mav, "what can I do for you?"

"You can stop running away."

Me? I'm the one running away? As if.

He reaches for me, and I bat his hands away. He sighs. "I'm done playing around Juniper. I want you. You want me. It's time to see where this can go."

I know exactly where it will go. It's this place I refer to as heartbreak city. No thanks.

"Not interested," I tell him before marching away.

D.E. Haggerty
Love and Laughter in Every Chapter

About the Author

D.E. Haggerty is an American who has spent the majority of her adult life abroad. She has lived in Istanbul, various places throughout Germany, and currently finds herself in The Hague. She has been a military policewoman, a lawyer, a B&B owner/operator and now a writer.

Made in United States
Troutdale, OR
04/04/2025